Pakistani Folk Tales: Toontoony Pie & Other Stories

Pakistani Folk Tales:

Toontoony Pie and Other Stories

Ashraf Siddiqui and Marilyn Lerch
Illustrated by Jan Fairservis

Hippocrene Books, Inc.
New York

To all the children of the world

This edition © 1998 by Hippocrene Books, Inc.

Originally published in 1961 by
The World Publishing Company.

All rights reserved.

For information address:
HIPPOCRENE BOOKS
171 Madison Avenue
New York, NY 10016

*Cataloging-in-Publication Data available from
the Library of Congress.*

ISBN 0-7818-0703-4

Printed in the United States of America.

Contents

Introduction   7

Toontoony pie   15

The rat who made one bargain
    too many   23

The tiger in the palanquin   32

Kashi and his wicked brothers   37

The crow and the sparrow   44

The fortune of the poet's son   50

The jackal and the crocodile   55

The two misers   61

The farmer's old horse   65

The gift of the holy man   70

The poor weaver and
    the princess   82

The man who was only
    three inches tall   91

Toontoony and the barber 98
The clever jackal and how
    he outwitted the tiger 104
The monkey, the tiger, and
    the jackal family 109
The tale of a Pakistan parrot 114
The crow and the grain of corn 124
The jackal with the torn nose 130
Four friends 136
The old woman and the thief 140
The ruby prince 144
The storyteller 155

Introduction

Pakistan is a new country—it was partitioned from India and made independent August 15, 1947—but it is an ancient land and its civilization is very old. Long before the Christian Era the regions of the Punjab, Sind, Baluchistan, Kashmir, and the Northwest Frontier of India—now West Pakistan—were the homes of many different kinds of people. Other people spread across India, and some of them settled in Bengal, now East Pakistan.

Among the most ancient people in India were the Aryans, who were ethnically related to many European races. They came from central Asia, down through the same mountain passes used by later invaders, including the Greeks led by Alexander the Great, the Persians, and the Moslems, who ruled most of India for many centuries. And finally, much later, after Vasco da Gama opened the sea route to India, came the Portuguese, the Dutch, the French, and the English, the last rulers of India.

All of these people left their mark on the life and civilization of India, for of course they brought with them their own ways of thinking, their arts, their religions, their weapons and clothing; and gradually these customs

7

and beliefs were absorbed into Indian life. Pakistan itself came into being as a new, independent country because most of the people who live in the regions that are now East and West Pakistan believe in Islam, the religious faith of the Moslems.

But of course all of these many different people were also affected by India and Indian ways of life as well, and often they took back to their own countries stories and ideas and ways of doing things they had learned in India. And this is one of the reasons that some of the tales in this book are similar to folk tales told in Western lands.

Since ancient times the people of India have loved to tell stories to their children. Eighty per cent of the people in Pakistan live in villages and earn their bread by farming. In the evenings they tell stories to their children, tales which they themselves heard from their parents when they were young. In many parts of the country there are professional storytellers, too, who travel from village to village telling stories that have been repeated from generation to generation since time immemorial. *The Panchatantra,* a very famous collection of Indo-Pakistani beast fables, is believed to have been written in 500 A.D.

In the early nineteenth century, many European scholars of folklore, including Jakob Grimm, believed that many of the basic themes of folk tales spread to Europe from India. Theodor Benfey, the German scholar who translated and published *The Panchatantra* in Europe in 1859, traced the origin of folklore themes to India and believed

8

that they spread to European countries through oral tradition and writings. Whether or not this can be proven, modern scholars of folklore recognize the importance of Indo-Pakistani folklore as a source for the folk tales of many European countries. Compare "The Four Friends" in this collection with the familiar Grimm retelling, "Bremen Town Musicians," and you will see how similar they are.

Most Pakistani folk tales are humorous, and birds and beasts that are familiar to India play an important part in them. The toontoony bird is a popular hero; in stories it is always plucky and resourceful, and able to outwit barbers or kings with ease. This bird, usually black with a yellow beak and a yellow patch on its neck, is a singing bird and can be tamed. With proper training, it may even be taught to repeat a few words of human speech. Many tales about it are popular in Pakistan; there are at least a hundred variations of the first story in this book still current in East Pakistan. "Toontoony and the Barber" is also popular in East Pakistan; hundreds of years ago, barbers acted as doctors for certain small operations, and so the toontoony was right in going to him for help in removing the thorn.

Jackals also appear in many Indo-Pakistani folk tales. There are at least fifty variations of "The Jackal with the Torn Nose" still told in East Pakistan today; such stories about this cunning fellow as "The Monkey, the Tiger, and the Jackal Family," "The Clever Jackal and How He

Outwitted the Tiger," and "The Tiger in the Palanquin" are also well-loved.

Princes and princesses, giants and ogres, magic and enchantment, are equally important; "The Gift of the Holy Man" is a typical East Pakistani story of magic. "The Two Misers" is probably of Arabic origin and might have been brought to India by Moslem traders.

All of the stories in this book are still told and retold in East and West Pakistan today. Sometimes a portion of the story is changed or omitted in the retelling. Sometimes new stories evolve out of an older one which has been told for centuries. Most of the tales in this book are known in both parts of Pakistan, although they are fourteen hundred miles apart. Five of them—"The Crow and the Grain of Corn," "The Rat Who Made One Bargain Too Many," "The Ruby Prince," "The Jackal and the Crocodile," "The Clever Jackal and How He Outwitted the Tiger"—are West Pakistani tales. All of these are based on Flora Annie Steel's retellings in *Tales of the Punjab,* which closely follow oral versions heard in Pakistani villages today.

In the evenings, when the work of the day is finished and families assemble, children in Pakistan like to recite this nonsense verse:

"What's the story?"
"The story of a frog."
"What kind of frog?"
"A lean frog . . ."

as a sign to mothers, or fathers, or grandmothers, that they are ready for a story. Those included here are only a few of the most popular ones still told in my country of Pakistan. There are hundreds of them, in hundreds of variations, but storytellers can tell only so many stories at one time.

One of the best ways to end is with another nonsense verse of Pakistan:

> "Here my story ends
> The notē plant bends . . ."

—*Ashraf Siddiqui*
Dacca, East Pakistan

What is the story?
>*The story of a frog.*

What kind of frog?
>*A lean frog.*

How lean?
>*As lean as a Brahmin.*

What kind of Brahmin?
>*A very good Brahmin.*

How good?
>*As good as a little monkey.*

What kind of monkey?
>*A monkey in the jungle.*

What kind of jungle?
>*A beautiful jungle.*

How beautiful?
>*As beautiful as the face of a child.*

Whose child?
>*His, who is lucky.*

Toontoony pie

Once upon a time there was a king in a far, far country. He lived in a luxurious palace surrounded by pools of clear blue water. Around the pools were beautiful gardens with many kinds of flowers and plants and trees.

Among the trees was a very tall one, and in that tree lived a warbler bird whose name was Toontoony.

Toontoony lived happily in his nest. He sang when he felt like singing and slept when he felt like sleeping. He found good things to eat, such as rice patties and mustard, in the king's courtyard, and Toontoony ate to his heart's content.

15

Usually he ate too much; then he always flew to his nest and took a nap.

Now, one day, here is what happened!

The king had so much money that twice a week he aired it on the palace roof to keep it from becoming rusty. Toontoony saw the money and thought that he would like to store some of it in his nest and become rich like the king. So he flew to the roof and took a golden coin.

Next morning he began to sing:

> The riches the king has in his chest,
> I also have here in my nest.

His majesty, the king, was sitting on his throne discussing important matters with messengers and ambassadors from foreign courts. The court was always full of ministers, commanders, tenants, servants, and what not.

The naughty bird continued to sing:

> The riches the king has in his chest,
> I also have here in my nest.

Some of the noblemen and servants began laughing behind the king's back, and he became very annoyed at the bird's song. After the court

16

was dismissed, the king ordered one of his servants to climb Toontoony's tree and see what riches he had in his nest.

The servant found the one golden coin and brought it to the king. All the time Toontoony was watching from another tree.

Next morning the affairs of state were conducted as usual. Toontoony began to dance and sing:

> Thief, thief, the king's a thief,
> He has stolen Toony's riches
> And brought him great grief!

The king blushed with shame and became furious because all the courtiers were laughing at him.

When the court was dismissed, the king ordered an attendant to capture the naughty bird. A trap was set and soon Toontoony was snared.

The king smiled triumphantly and rubbed his hands together in glee. "Now what will happen?" asked the king. "Who will save you, naughty bird?"

The king's seven daughters were present when Toontoony was caught. The king handed the bird

17

to his eldest daughter and told her to cook it in
a pie for his supper.

The seven daughters each wanted to fondle
Toontoony. At last it was the youngest daughter's
turn, but she held the bird so gently that he was
able to fly away.

The other daughters scolded the youngest for
her carelessness. "When our father finds out that
the bird has escaped, he will hang us!" they cried.

What to do? What could be done?

The eldest daughter was the wisest and most
experienced. "It is no use crying over spilt milk,"
she said to her sisters. "Let us do something.
There are many frogs in the pools. We shall catch
one secretly and cook it for the king. He will
think that it is Toontoony and won't hang us."

The king came to dinner in high spirits and ate
the frog with zest. He addressed the frog, thinking
that it was Toontoony, "Now, naughty bird, will
you fly away? Will you humiliate me again?"

The next day the king had just sat down on his throne when Toontoony began to sing:

> Listen, courtiers, hi!
> What a lie, what a lie!
> The king ate frog pie
> Thinking it was I!

Now it was against the king's religion to eat a frog, and besides frogs are unwholesome creatures.

The king was astonished and humiliated. He hastened to his bedchamber. On the way he met his youngest daughter and demanded to know what had happened to Toontoony. When his frightened daughter broke down and confessed the whole story, the king grew red in the face with rage. He called his seven daughters before him and with a sharp sword cut off their ears.

While the king sat in court the next day the naughty bird sang even more joyously.

> What a lie! What a lie!
> The king wanted Toontoony pie,
> And instead he ate a frog fry.
>
> Then what happened? Ha, ha, hear.
> Seven daughters lost their ears.

The king became so angry that he chased everyone from the court and ordered his attendants to catch the naughty bird by hook or by crook. The attendants pursued Toony all day and finally caught him.

The king seized the bird with both hands and ordered a servant to bring a pot of boiling water. He told a soldier to be ready with a sharp sword so that he could kill Toony if he tried to fly away.

The king doused Toony in the boiling water a couple of times, but he was so eager to be rid of the troublesome bird that he decided to swallow him whole. When the king swallowed Toontoony, a remarkable thing happened. The bird came out through the king's right nostril and flew away. The soldier swung his sword; but, unfortunately, instead of killing Toony, he cut off the king's nose.

Next day Toontoony flew over the palace and sang this song:

> Tata ting tata ting
> See the wretched state of the king!
> He wanted to eat Toontoony pie
> But ate a frog instead, oh, my!

And then what happened? Ha, ha, hear
Seven daughters lost their ears,
To bring my story to a close,
I caused the king to lose his nose!

Tata ting tata ting
Noseless king!
Noseless king!

Toontoony sang this song over and over and then flew away toward another country never to be heard of again.

The rat who made one bargain too many

Once upon a time there was a plump rat who was very kind and also very shrewd. He was walking along the road one day when he found a thick branch under a pile of brush. He put it into his sack to use for winter kindling.

A short time later he came upon an old man trying in vain to light a fire. Around the man were clustered three little girls crying piteously. The rat, who never saw suffering without attempting to help, called out, "Poor fellow, is there anything I can do to aid you?"

"Perhaps you can, Mr. Rat. My children are hungry. The wood is wet from the spring rains, and I can't build a fire to cook their meager breakfast."

23

"See what I have here," said the kind rat. "This dry stick will soon make a fine blaze."

The poor man was overjoyed; and to show his appreciation, he gave the rat a bit of dough.

The rat trotted off, thinking that he was very shrewd to have gotten a week's supply of food for one dry stick.

Further on, the rat heard a terrible noise. He entered the yard of a pottery maker and found two little boys crying as if their hearts would break.

"There, there, don't cry," said the kindhearted rat. "Perhaps I can help you. Tell me what is the matter."

The eldest boy wiped the tears from his eyes and whimpered, "Our parents went to the village to get food this morning; but they are late in returning, and we are so hungry that our stomachs hurt."

"Well, my children, take this bit of dough and bake it. In a few minutes everything will be all right."

The children thanked him a hundred times. "Here, Mr. Rat," said the eldest, "take this pot which my father made yesterday. We shall not forget your kindness."

The rat tottered off with the heavy pot on his back. It is a trifle cumbersome, he thought, but worth much more than the bit of dough. Yes, indeed, I am a shrewd hand at bargaining.

By and by the rat came upon a funny scene. An old farmer was milking a buffalo, but as he did not have a pail, he was draining the milk into a pair of shoes. Now the rat was not only kind and shrewd, but also very clean.

"Mr. Farmer, when the milk comes from the buffalo, it is clean. You are making it dirty by using those shoes. A pail would be much better."

"A pail would be much better," said the farmer, mimicking the rat. "Of course, a pail would be better, if I *had* one."

"Well, you do have one. Use mine. I cannot stand dirty milk."

The farmer thanked the rat and soon had the pot brimming full of cool, clean milk. "Here, my little friend, have a taste of this refreshing milk."

The rat sat back on his haunches and pulled

25

at his whiskers. "No, I deserve a better bargain than that. You could not have sold the milk because it was dirty, therefore the buffalo was worth nothing to you. I think that you should give me the buffalo in exchange for the pot."

The farmer laughed heartily. "And just what can a little fellow like you do with this huge animal?"

The rat drew up to his full stature and puffed out his chest. "Never mind. I'll handle the buffalo."

The farmer, who enjoyed practical jokes, tied the buffalo's halter around the neck of the rat.

The rat set off in a cocky manner, but he had only walked a few yards when the rope began to choke him. Turning around, he saw that the buffalo had stopped by the roadside to graze. The

26

rat pulled and tugged and shouted, but, of course, the buffalo could not be budged.

Well, rationalized the rat, this stubborn monster is my property now, and I must take good care of him. So I shall follow him. He knows better than I where the good grazing is.

All day long the buffalo wandered from one grassy spot to another, dragging the poor rat behind him. And you can imagine how fast the little rat's legs had to move in order to keep pace with the rambling buffalo. At twilight the buffalo lay down by a cool stream, and the weary rat gratefully sank down beside him.

A few minutes later a wedding procession stopped by the stream to rest. It seems that a prospective bride was being carried to meet her bridegroom. The four bride-bearers built a fire and began cooking a bit of rice.

"A fine thing," grumbled one of them, "to carry our heavy burden all day in the hot sun and then have only this bit of rice to eat."

The rat listened to every word. Suddenly an idea came to him that would lead him out of his difficulties.

"My friends," piped up the rat, "I know what it is to be hungry. Please take my buffalo and cook him for your supper."

The four bearers laughed and laughed at the thought of a rat owning a buffalo, but they were too hungry to argue. They killed the buffalo, and in a few minutes a large steak was sizzling over the fire. After they had gorged themselves on the tasty meat, they offered a morsel to the rat.

"Now, wait a minute," cried the rat, puffing out his chest. "I am a shrewd bargainer. Why only today I traded a stick for a week's supply of food.

I traded the food for a pot. For the pot I received this buffalo. So, I shall take nothing less this time than the bride herself."

The bearers, realizing the trouble they had gotten into, shook with fear and decided that the best thing to do was flee, which they did in a great rush.

The rat, chuckling to himself, walked over to the covered litter and lifted the curtain. He drew back in amazement, for inside sat the loveliest lady he had ever seen. But the rat quickly regained his composure and in a sweet voice said, "My dear and lovely bride, you are mine now. Let me take you to my abode."

It was growing dark and the young bride, frightened at being alone in the great woods, gratefully accepted the rat's offer.

When they arrived at the rat's hole, he jumped in and graciously offered his hand to the bride. She giggled and did not move one inch.

"Well, come along," urged the rat. "You are mine now and must follow me."

The bride giggled again and said, "Do you expect me to squeeze into that tiny hole?"

The rat sat back on his haunches and pulled

29

at his whiskers. At last he said, "Yes, it is obvious that you are overfed and that I must enlarge my hole in order to accommodate you. In the meantime you can sleep under this plum tree."

"I cannot sleep if I am hungry," complained the bride.

The rat, grumbling to himself that brides were terribly bothersome, disappeared into his hole and came up a few minutes later with two peas.

"Gracious," cried the bride, "do you expect me to clean house, cook, and sew on two peas a day!"

The rat sighed and shook his head. It was more than he had bargained for. "Tonight I shall gather some wild plums, and tomorrow you can carry a basketful to market and sell them to buy the delicacies that you desire."

The next day, the bride, dressed in her lovely gown, wandered through the village streets selling plums. She came to the palace gates, and lo and behold! there was the bride's mother, the queen, running toward her. They embraced amid much weeping. Just then the rat appeared. "I demand my wife," he yelled, jumping up and down. "I traded a buffalo for her, and she belongs to me!"

The clever queen could scarcely keep from laughing. "My dear Son-in-law," she said sweetly, "do not be angry. We have just finished preparing a warm, spacious room for you. Come. Follow me!"

The rat, delighted beyond all measure, followed the queen. She led him to the stove, opened the oven door, and announced, "Here it is, dear Son-in-law, hop in."

The rat did so in one leap, and bang! the oven door was slammed in his face. He sat there tugging at his whiskers and daydreaming about his good fortune. But the room was getting a bit stuffy. He rapped on the door and asked if a window could be raised. Outside, he heard the queen and the bride laughing hysterically. The room became hotter and hotter, and soon his tail began to sizzle.

"Oh! I have been tricked!" cried the rat. "I shall never, never, never make another bargain."

On hearing this, the queen opened the door, and the rat leaped out. He had learned his lesson, and he never, never, never made another bargain.

The tiger in the palanquin

Once upon a time, there was a tiger whose nephew
was a jackal. Now the jackal is known to be a very
cunning animal. And sometimes even his friends
cannot trust him.

The tiger and the jackal often traveled together,
living off the wild flesh that the tiger killed.

One day the jackal invited his uncle to dinner.
When the tiger came, the jackal requested him to
sit down. He then left, saying that he had to call
his other guests and that he would be back in a
short time.

Minute after minute, hour after hour passed,
but no jackal. When midnight came, the tiger left
quite vexed. He resolved to teach his nephew a
lesson.

The next day the tiger invited the jackal to
lunch. When the jackal sat down at the dinner
table, he was served sticks and bare bones. The

tiger was eating enthusiastically and inquired, "Nephew, how do you like your lunch?"

The jackal replied, "It is very good, almost as good as the meal which you had at my home last night." The jackal was very angry, but refused to show it.

A few days later, the jackal found a field of sugar cane and began eating greedily. When his stomach could hold no more, he gathered an armful to take home. The farmer who had planted the field saw all this and decided to teach the jackal a lesson. With planks and bamboo sticks he made a trap which resembled a palanquin. A *palanquin* is an enclosed litter which is carried on the shoulders of four bearers. Only the wealthy can afford to be conveyed in this manner.

The jackal watched the farmer preparing the trap and decided to play a joke on his uncle.

He went to the tiger and said most respectfully, "Hello, Uncle. Since I last saw you, I have fallen into good fortune. I moved to a new home several miles from here. The people are kind and generous, so generous that they gave me a whole acre of land thriving with sweet sugar cane.

Venerable Uncle, how would you like to accompany me to my new home and partake of this delicacy?"

When the tiger heard "sugar cane," he immediately agreed to go. Then the jackal made up another lie. He said that the king of the country had invited him to the marriage of his daughter, the princess. "The king is sending a royal palanquin to convey me to the ceremony. Won't you come along?"

The tiger was flattered and wanted to leave for his nephew's home at once.

When they reached the sugar-cane field, the jackal told his uncle to eat as much as he wanted. The tiger ate all the juicy stalks that he could hold and then inquired about the palanquin.

"Ah," said the cunning jackal, "it has already arrived. Follow me!" He led the tiger to the palanquin which had been built by the farmer to trap the jackal.

The tiger said, "Well, here is the palanquin, but where are the bearers?"

The jackal replied, "Do not worry. The bearers

are on their way. Please get inside and I shall wait
for them here."

The foolish tiger jumped into the palanquin,
and the trap door slammed tightly shut.

The mischievous jackal shouted, "Uncle, why
did you close the door? Let me in."

The tiger answered sneeringly, "You need not enter. I, alone, shall enjoy the royal marriage. Ha, ha, ha."

Smiling craftily, the jackal said, "Well, that is not very gracious of you after my hospitality, but have it your own way."

Just then the farmer arrived, carrying a big stick. Thinking that the trapped tiger was the jackal, he beat him until he was dead. The jackal watched from a distance and then dashed into the forest, laughing to himself.

Kashi and his wicked brothers

Once upon a time, there was a family of seven boys. Six of them had married and lived away from home. The youngest, Kashi, was not married. On him was lavished most of the father's great wealth. For this reason Kashi's brothers hated him. The day came when their jealousy boiled over and they agreed to get rid of Kashi.

They visited their youngest brother and proposed to find a bride for him. Although Kashi was innocent and kind, he was also very shrewd; he saw treachery in his brothers' hearts, but decided to go along with their plan.

A few days later he was told that a bride had been found and that the wedding was to take place the next evening at the house of the girl's father. Kashi knew that his brothers were up to no good, but he could not pass up a chance to outwit them, so he agreed to go.

37

The next day the seven brothers, all riding fine horses, set off for the bride's home. Just before they were to cross a wide and turbulent river, Kashi abruptly reined in his horse. "My brothers, I have forgotten the most important thing for the wedding and must go home to fetch it. Wait for me here!"

The brothers were angry and impatient, but they could not show their feelings, so they dismounted and waited on the bank of the river.

Meanwhile, Kashi, the clever one, found a cowherd and boldly asked him if he wished to marry the loveliest girl in the kingdom. The young and foolish cowherd quickly said yes. Then Kashi exchanged clothes with him, telling him where to find the brothers and how to act.

It was dark when the cowherd found the six brothers. They were so eager to carry out their evil plot that they did not notice the change. The cowherd was led to a boat, and in midstream he was ruthlessly tossed overboard.

In the meantime, Kashi drove home the cattle and waited for his brothers to return. You can imagine the look of bewilderment and surprise that lit their faces when the six brothers rode into the yard. But they quickly composed themselves and said, "Ah, dear Brother, what a great relief it is to see you alive. We thought surely that the waters of the wild river had stifled your last breath. Let us embrace you, favored one. By the way, where did you get those cows?"

"As I was struggling in the water, dear Brothers, I bumped against a large brown hump. It turned out to be a cow. I clung to its back, and it carried me safely to shore. Once there, a god appeared and told me that if I repeated a magic word nine times, I would receive nine fine cows. And you see, it came true."

The six brothers, defeated for the moment but more determined than ever to rid themselves of Kashi, trudged to their homes. The next night they carried torches to his home and burned it to the ground.

But Kashi was not in the house. He had visited a friend for the night. When he returned and found his home nothing but a heap of ashes, he immediately turned his misfortune to advantage. Taking a gunny sack, he filled it with the charcoal and started off for the village market.

Before reaching the charcoal stand, he met a man who carried a gunny sack exactly like his. "What do you have in that bag, sir?" asked Kashi.

The man looked around and then whispered in Kashi's ear, "A sackful of rupees."

"Ah," said the clever Kashi, "and in mine I have gold nuggets."

Kashi arranged for the two of them to stay in the same inn that night. When he fell asleep the stranger crept out of bed, substituted his bag for Kashi's, and made his escape feeling very happy

and clever. Now, Kashi had suspected the man's intentions all along. He awoke early, looked in his bag and, sure enough, found it full of rupees.

Delighted with his success, he headed home, and on the way concocted a new plan to torment his brothers. He spread the rupees on the ground in his front yard and used a corn measure to count them. Then he placed all but one in a heavy chest.

This one rupee he left in a conspicuous spot in his yard and waited for his brothers to visit him. When the brothers saw the rupee, their jealousy increased tenfold. They asked Kashi with hypocritical gentleness where he had gotten the money.

"Oh, my good Brothers, it is simply that I have a knack for turning misfortune into blessings. My house burned down, you know, and by selling the charcoal that I salvaged, I earned a great deal of money."

"Dear Kashi, if you tell us your secret for making money, we could all be rich and live happily ever after."

"There is no secret, Brothers. I will gladly share my good fortune with you. A few miles from here is a village where charcoal is very hard to obtain. The people need it so badly that they give one bag of rupees for every bag of charcoal. I suggest that tonight you all burn down your homes, collect the charcoal, sell it, and presto! you will be rich men."

That night the rapacious brothers set fire to their homes, gathered the charcoal, and set off for Kashi's imaginary village. They came to a village and decided that this was the right one according to Kashi's description. Confident of becoming rich men in a few hours, they walked up and down the streets calling out, "We have the best charcoal in the kingdom. One bag is worth one bag of rupees. Who will buy?"

A crowd gathered and began following the foolish brothers. At first the villagers laughed and ridiculed the vendors. Then they became angry when the brothers refused to stop their silly chatter, and finally chased them out of town.

The dejected, defeated brothers decided that the best thing to do was return home and forget their silly idea. Then they remembered that they had no homes to return to and no clothing and no food.

In this pitiful condition, they were forced to become servants in their village. Kashi's good luck continued. He married into a wealthy family and gave liberally to his brothers. He even invited them to live with him. Through Kashi's willingness to forgive those who intended him harm, he became an honored and respected man among his brothers and his people.

The crow and the sparrow

Once a sparrow made friends with a crow. The crow came to the house of the sparrow almost every day and said, "Hello, friend. How are you?"

And the sparrow always answered, "Fine. How are you? Please have a seat."

The sparrow was friendly and sincere; the crow was greedy and mischievous.

One day when they were hunting for food, the crow spied some red peppers in a farmer's yard. The farmer had spread the peppers on a mat to dry in the sun. The crow said to the sparrow,

44

"My friend, see how many red peppers there are! Let us go and eat."

While they were eating, the crow inquired, "My friend, how do you like the food?"

And the sparrow replied, "Oh, very much."

"Would you like to play a game?" asked the crow.

"Indeed, I would," replied the sparrow.

"Let us divide the remaining peppers equally between us and see which of us can eat the most."

"I have no objection," answered the sparrow.

"But suppose you are defeated? What will you give me?"

The good-natured sparrow replied, "Whatever you want."

"All right," said the crow, "the one who wins will eat the meat of the other."

The sparrow agreed, because he thought that the crow was joking with him. Can one friend eat the meat of the other?

The crow ate one pepper and hid three under the mat. The sparrow ate each pepper fairly.

After an hour the crow said, "Look, my friend,

45

I have eaten all of my peppers, but you have not eaten even half of your portion."

The sparrow laughed and replied, "All right, you are the winner."

The crow reminded him that the winner was to receive a prize. The sparrow laughed and said, "What prize do you want? Tell me."

The crow reminded him of their bet and demanded the sparrow's meat.

At last, the sparrow came to his senses and realized that the crow was serious. "Since you really demand my meat," said the sparrow, "I will be true to my agreement. But before that, I have one request. Everyone knows that you are an unclean bird and that you eat lots of dirty things with your beak. If you want my meat, you must wash your beak."

The crow went to the river and cried:

> River! River! Give me water.
> I shall wash my beak, make myself neat,
> And eat the sweet sparrow's meat!

The river replied, "You want water? Very well, I have no objection. But everyone says that you eat many unclean things. So if you want to wash your beak in my water, you must get a pot and then you can have as much water as you want."

The crow went to the pottery maker in the village.

> Potter! Potter! Give me a pot.
> I will fetch water from the river,
> Wash my beak, make myself neat,
> And eat the sweet sparrow's meat!

The pottery maker replied, "You want a pot? I do not object, but I have no clay. If you bring me some clay, I will make a pot."

The crow went to a field and began digging up clay with his beak. The earth said, "The whole world knows that you eat rubbish and unclean things. I cannot permit you to dig my clay unless you use a spade."

The crow went to the village blacksmith. The old blacksmith was sitting idly in his shop with an unlit hubble-bubble in his hand.

The crow said:

Blacksmith! Blacksmith! Give me a spade.
I will dig up the earth, take clay to the potter to make
    a pot,
Fetch water in the pot and wash my beak to make
    myself neat,
So that I can eat the sweet sparrow's meat.

The blacksmith replied, "You want a spade? That is all right with me, but, you see, I have no fire in my forge. So if you want me to make a spade, you must bring me some fire."

The crow went to a farmer's house near-by. The wife of the farmer was cooking rice in the courtyard. The crow cried:

Dear farmer's wife! Give me fire,
Iwill take the fire to the blacksmith, who will make
    me a spade.
I will take the spade and dig some clay,
Take the clay and give it to the pottery maker to make
    a pot.
I will take the pot,
Go to the river, wash my beak,

Make myself neat,
And eat the sweet sparrow's meat.

The farmer's wife replied, "You want fire? All right. I do not have the least objection to giving you fire. But the question is, how will you carry it?"

"Put it on my back," said the crow.

The farmer's wife put the fire upon the back of the crow, and immediately his feathers caught fire. The greedy crow was burnt to ashes. And the honest sparrow lived to a ripe old age.

The fortune of the poet's son

A long, long time ago in a faraway country, there lived a great poet. Throughout the land the poet was famous for his knowledge of literature and his beautiful poems, but still he was not content, for his son was very stupid. The son never read books nor did he love beautiful things, and this hurt the poet deeply.

The poet soon passed away, convinced that his son would always be ignorant. By and by the rich inheritance that the poet had left was squandered, and the wife and son went hungry. All the neighbors of the son constantly rebuked him for his stupidity and laziness and told him to ask the king for help.

But how could the son go to the imperial court? He was neither wise nor talented like his father. How could he gain the king's respect?

Finally, however, after repeated admonishments

from his neighbors, the son decided to go to the court. All along the way he trembled at the though of speaking to the king, and many times he was ready to return home. Just before he reached the palace, he sat down under a banyan tree to rest.

A few cowherds were playing near-by while their oxen grazed in the meadow. It had rained a short time before and the grazing place was covered by muddy water. One ox was fruitlessly beating his hoofs in the water, trying to find the lush grass. The poet's son saw this and suddenly composed these unpoetical lines:

> You're stirring the water foolishly, friend,
> And splashing drops in the breeze.
> I know what you're trying to do.
> I know with the greatest of ease.

The son felt more confident after composing the bad poem and went directly to the palace. There, he was informed that the royal barber was shaving the king and that this was an improper time to gain an audience with his majesty. But the poet's son was so impatient to finish the ordeal that he demanded admittance anyway.

When the king learned that the son of his good friend, the famous poet, wished to see him, he immediately called him hither. The king asked, "Do you write poetry as well as your father?"

The son became flustered. He hesitated and then stuttered, "Yes . . . no . . . I mean, not quite as good."

The king thought that the son was shy and that his shyness was a sign of modesty.

"Come, come, dear son of my friend, recite some of your poetry."

The poor, embarrassed son began to tremble. He did not know what to do. Finally, in his

nervous state, he turned to the barber instead of the king and repeated his bad lines:

> You're stirring the water foolishly, friend,
> And splashing drops in the breeze.
> I know what you're trying to do.
> I know with the greatest of ease.

As soon as the poet's son had finished reciting his poem, the barber fell prostrate at the feet of the king, and with tears in his eyes, begged for mercy.

Of course, the king was astonished at this ridiculous act. "What in the world is the matter?" demanded the king.

The barber cried out, "I am not guilty, Your Majesty. I was bribed by the queen to do so."

"To do what?" asked the king angrily.

The barber then confessed that the queen had given him a great sum of money to use his sharp razor to murder the king. But when the barber heard the poem of the poet's son, he thought that the son knew of his evil intentions, and so he confessed, hoping that the king would be lenient.

The king, in a great rage, demanded the queen's presence. When he accused her of the evil plot, she broke down and said that it was all true!

The queen's nose was cut off, and she was exiled to the forest where wild beasts devoured her. The king rewarded the poet's son with ten bags of gold. Thus, the son became exceedingly rich.

In triumph he returned home and shortly after, married the daughter of a wealthy merchant. He and his bride and his mother lived happily ever after.

The jackal and the crocodile

One day, handsome Mr. Jackal, feeling very care-free and mischievous, was walking beside a wide, deep stream. He spied a ripe, heavily laden plum tree across the stream. Unable to reach the fruit, he naturally desired it more than anything else in the world.

Just then Miss Crocodile floated into sight. There was a proud, disdainful look upon her face.

"Dear Miss Crocodile," said the jackal, smiling to himself, "you are growing lovelier each day. Won't you stop awhile and chat? If only I could swim, I would gather those lush plums for you and we would dine together."

Now Miss Crocodile was very susceptible to flattery, and the jackal's warm words sent thrills up and down her scales. But she was a coy one.

"Mr. Jackal, I could not possibly dine with you

unless . . ."—she hesitated and blushed green all over—"unless you desire to marry me."

The jackal laughed roguishly. "Aha! This is my lucky day! I shall be delighted to marry you. Now, my fair love, just gather those delicious plums and we shall celebrate our coming wedding. Then I'll go to the barber, who will arrange the grandest wedding imaginable."

Miss Crocodile crossed the stream, gathered the choicest plums, and eagerly carried them back to her beloved. She was so excited that she could

not eat one bite, but Mr. Jackal ate until his
stomach bulged.

"And now, my love, though it grieves me to
leave you for one moment, I must find the barber.
It is very far, you know, so do not worry if I am
gone for a long time." And with that he kissed
her cheek and bounded into the forest.

For a few days Miss Crocodile idled by the
plum tree, dreaming about Mr. Jackal and their

coming wedding. But when two weeks passed and her beloved did not return, she realized that she had been tricked. She swore to revenge her injured pride.

The next day she hid herself beneath the bank of a shallow pool where the jackal often came to drink and bathe. Soon he rambled out of the forest, singing to himself in a happy-go-lucky manner, and jumped into the middle of the pool. Miss Crocodile reached out blindly and grabbed the jackal's leg. He guessed who it was, and a scheme quickly came to his shrewd mind.

"My dearest love," he cried, "I am drowning. Let go of that old root and save me."

When Miss Crocodile heard this, she let go of the jackal's leg. Then the freed jackal leaped onto the bank and roared with laughter.

"My love, my love," he chanted, "someday I shall find the barber." And he bounded into the woods.

Now Miss Crocodile was really furious. "He won't escape me another time," she said to herself angrily.

She found the jackal's home, a hole in the ground, and lay in hiding, waiting for him. As the jackal approached his abode, he discovered Miss Crocodile's tracks and followed them right up to his doorstep. In a voice loud enough for Miss Crocodile to hear, he said, "How strange that my wife is silent. When I come home, she always says:

> My handsome jackal so clever and smart,
> What have you brought to please my heart?"

On hearing this, Miss Crocodile sweetly repeated the jackal's limerick:

> My handsome jackal so clever and smart,
> What have you brought to please my heart?

The jackal put both paws over his mouth to keep from laughing out loud. Then he quietly entered his hole and saw Miss Crocodile lying in the corner, perfectly still. He took out a large handkerchief and began to sob. "Oh, look, my dear wife is dead. But wait a moment. Is she dead? I've always heard that dead people wag their tails."

And with that Miss Crocodile began to wag her tail. The jackal could no longer contain his laughter. He dashed outside and ran toward the woods, laughing and singing as he went:

> Yes, yes, it's true,
> Dead people do
> Wag their tails!

Miss Crocodile was so demoralized by Mr. Jackal's latest triumph that she never again tried to revenge herself. She finally learned that vanity is a false pose that calls forth ridicule.

The two misers

Once upon a time there were two misers who lived in the same village. Their miserly way of living was so legendary that everyone for miles around knew them by name. A rumor spread that went like this: If anyone saw either of the misers in the morning, he would suffer many difficulties during the day. And, if anyone uttered the misers' names, his day would be passed in fruitless endeavor. Because of this rumor, everyone avoided the company of the two misers.

Since they had no friends, the two misers were forced to seek each other's company and spend their days in idle gossip.

One day the elder miser said to the younger, "Friend, everyone in the village and surrounding country knows that we are misers. We are never invited to ceremonies or family festivals, which I enjoy very much. I have a great desire to have

61

a fine dinner of my own and invite you as my special and only guest."

The younger miser readily accepted the invitation. On the appointed day, he entered the humble home of the elder miser, who inquired what foods his guest most enjoyed.

The younger miser answered, "I have heard that the milk bread made in our village is the best in the country, but never in my life have I tasted it. If you do not object, my friend, I would like to have some."

The elder miser said that he would be delighted to buy milk bread for his guest. They went to the village bread shop, and the elder miser asked the shopkeeper, "Tell me, is your milk bread sweet and soft?"

The shopkeeper replied, "Why, sir, this is the sweetest milk bread in the country, and it is as soft as butter."

Now the elder miser knew that butter cost less money than milk bread; so he suggested that they buy butter, which, he explained, was more tasty anyway.

At the butter shop, the owner brought out the

62

best butter on his shelf. The elder miser asked,
"How do you know that this is the finest butter
in the country? Is it as smooth as oil?"

The owner hesitated and then said, "Well, sir,
honestly it is not as smooth as oil, but . . ."

"Well, then," interrupted the elder miser, "it is
not the finest butter in the country, and I do not
want it on my table. Come, friend, oil will make
a more tasty meal, don't you think?"

And, without giving the younger miser a chance
to answer, the other rushed him from the shop.

They found a shop where oil was sold. The elder miser asked, "How is your oil, shopkeeper? Is it of the best quality?"

"See for yourself, sir. It is as clear as the water in yonder river."

"Ah, yes, water!" cried the elder miser. "Certainly water is the most healthful thing that one can drink." And with that he took his guest to the river and graciously told him to drink as much water as he wanted.

The farmer's old horse

There was once a farmer who owned a horse. The horse worked hard day and night for the farmer, and as a result he became weak and old before his time.

The farmer noticed that his horse was becoming more worthless each day and thought it best to get rid of the weary animal. So one day the farmer told the horse to leave and to devise his own means of support. The horse was astonished and deeply grieved at the farmer's command. Where could an old overworked horse go and make a living?

The horse begged his master to reconsider his decision and to remember all the hard work that he had done for him. The master replied, "I shall only reconsider after you have brought home a live tiger that you have captured yourself."

Had anybody ever heard of such a thing? A horse catching a tiger?

With a heavy heart, the horse wandered into the forest, and growing tired, sat down under a tree to rest. Just then a jackal came by and said, "Hello, Cousin. Why are you alone in the forest? Why have you left your farm?"

The unhappy horse proceeded to tell the sad story of his life.

The jackal encouraged him by saying, "You need not worry. The farmer commanded you to bring back a living tiger, right? A living lion would impress him even more, don't you think?"

Now, it so happened that recently a lion had come to the forest and was slaughtering all the animals to satisfy his immense hunger. The animals of the forest were horrified and angry, but as the lion is king of the beasts, nobody dared attack him.

The clever jackal had thought a long time about a way to snare the lion, and now he shared his plan with the horse.

"Lie down on the ground, Cousin, and pretend that you are dead. When I shout, '*Hukahua*,' jump up and run with all your strength back to your master's stable."

The jackal left the old horse lying in the middle of the path and eventually met the lion. He saluted the ferocious beast and exclaimed, "God save the king! How is the health of his majesty?"

The lion was flattered by the jackal's obsequiousness and decided not to harm him. Then the jackal said, "Your Highness, there is a dead horse lying in the pathway near-by. He would make a fine feast for the king of beasts. Won't you follow me, please?"

The jackal led the lion to the spot where the old horse was playing dead. The jackal turned to the lion and suggested, "Wouldn't it be a nice idea to carry the horse by its tail back to your den?"

"How is that possible?" asked the lion haughtily.

"It is not at all difficult, Sire," explained the jackal. "I shall tie the tail of the horse to your strong hind legs, and then you can easily carry him to your royal residence."

The lion liked the idea, and so the jackal tied the legs of the lion to the horse's tail. Then the jackal shouted, "*Hukahua!*"

As soon as the old horse heard the cry, he jumped up and galloped at full speed back to his master's stable. The farmer was struck dumb when he saw his old horse gallop into the yard, dragging a living, helpless lion behind him. The lion was caged and sold to the king for a high

price. The farmer was convinced that his faithful horse was still a valuable asset. From that time on, the horse lived happily with his master.

And in the forest the jackal and all the other animals breathed a sigh of relief, because the wicked lion could no longer harm them.

The gift of the holy man

In a certain country there once lived an extremely poor man. He was so poor that his family went without food most of the time. They did not have enough clothes to cover their bodies, and their home was in pitiable shape. The poor man was constantly chided by his wife and children for his worthlessness. One day he became tired of his dire poverty and decided that there was nothing left for him to do but wander into the forest and be devoured by wild beasts.

Soon after entering the forest, he came to a house and found a mendicant deeply absorbed in meditation near-by. The poor man, out of compassion, swept the courtyard of the mendicant and set his house in order. He also led the holy man's cow to pasture and fed it lush grass. He plucked some wild flowers, and after washing

70

them in pure water, placed them by the praying place of the mendicant.

When the holy man finished his meditations he opened his eyes, and the first thing he saw was the poor man. Then he discovered his house was neat and clean, his cow was well-fed, and he saw the delicate flowers. Now the mendicant was gifted with the power of foreknowledge. He knew immediately that the man standing before him was extremely poor, and he decided to help him.

The mendicant asked the poor man to sit by him. The poor man, with great humility, folded his hands and sat by the holy man.

"I know that you are very poor," said the mendicant. "But you will not remain poor if you follow my advice. I give you this handkerchief. One side of it is yellow, and the other side is green. If you spread the green side against the ground, you will receive gold coins. Now, take it and do not stop between this forest and your home. If you follow my advice, I am sure that you will never be poor again."

The grateful man salaamed the mendicant a hundred times and then set out for his home.

The day was extremely hot, and after he left the shade of the forest the scorching sun soon sapped the poor man's strength. He sat on the steps of a shop to rest. Out of curiosity he spread the green side of the handkerchief against the ground. And lo! a pile of golden coins appeared on the handkerchief.

The shopkeeper saw this wondrous thing happen before his eyes and devised a plan for cheating the poor man out of his wealth. He invited him into his chambers and feasted him with cakes and other sweets. The poor man was amazed and

flattered that such hospitality should be offered him.

During the dinner, the shopkeeper cunningly prodded the poor man into disclosing the secret of the handkerchief. The greedy shopkeeper then invited the poor man to spend the night, because he enjoyed so much the company of pious people who were favored by God.

The poor man accepted right away, and before going to bed, entrusted the handkerchief and gold coins to the shopkeeper. Several times he asked his host to guard the treasure zealously.

The next morning, the poor man prepared to continue his journey home and asked the shopkeeper to return the handkerchief and gold coins.

Imagine what happened! The clever shopkeeper had replaced the magic handkerchief with an ordinary one and now placed it reverently in the poor man's hands, along with the coins. Not suspecting any trickery, the poor man kindly thanked the shopkeeper a hundred times for his generosity and proceeded on his way.

The poor man reached home lighthearted and gay. The first thing he did was to shower the golden coins on his wife's lap. She was elated beyond words. All day long the poor man told the story of the magic handkerchief over and over again. At twilight, he gathered his family together and with a grand flourish spread the handkerchief on the ground. But nothing happened. He spread it again, waited . . . but nothing happened. He rubbed his eyes, laid the handkerchief down again . . . but still, nothing!

The wife thought that she had been brutally deceived, and she stormed and raged at her foolish husband. She accused him of stealing the coins from some rich man's coffers. She grabbed a broom and began beating the poor old man. At last he freed himself from her clutches, and suspecting that the friendly shopkeeper had been the cause of all this trouble, set off in that direction.

As soon as the poor man entered the shop, he accused the shopkeeper of stealing the magic handkerchief.

The shopkeeper pretended that never before in his life had he seen this impertinent man and drove him from the shop.

The poor man tore his hair and cried. Ah, the

74

mendicant had warned him not to stop on his way home. If only he had followed the holy man's advice. How could he face him now?

After much indecision, the poor man resolved to go back to the mendicant's house and ask for forgiveness. When he arrived there, he scrubbed the holy man's house and put everything in order. He fed the cow and picked wild flowers for the holy man's praying place.

When the mendicant opened his eyes, he said, "Do not worry, I know what has happened to you. You will recover the magic handkerchief."

The next morning the mendicant gave the poor man a thick stick and told him to visit the shop-keeper on his way home. "If you order the stick to beat someone, it will do so until you command it to stop."

The poor man realized that he had been given the magic stick to teach the shopkeeper a good lesson.

After salaaming the mendicant a hundred times, he set off for the shopkeeper's abode. Now the shopkeeper was clever enough to surmise that probably the stick which the poor man carried was magic, too, so he politely received the poor man and apologized for his previous misbehavior.

The poor man smiled, and feigning innocence, offered to have his magic stick perform. The shopkeeper's wife and children gathered around, and the poor man uttered these words:

> Stick, stick, holy man's stick,
> Beat them, beat them hard and quick.
> Teach these people that greed is wrong,
> Show them right is always strong!

And see! Wonder of wonders!

The stick began beating the shopkeeper and his family mercilessly. Unable to bear the violent blows, the wife took shelter in her room and the shopkeeper escaped to the roof. But the magic stick was all-knowing and everywhere at once. It doubtlessly would have killed them all had not the shopkeeper fallen prostrate at the poor man's feet and begged forgiveness.

The shopkeeper returned the magic handkerchief and swore a hundred times that he would never again commit such a terrible deed. Now, the poor man, with the magic handkerchief clutched in his hand, proceeded, hastened rather

76

. . . not hastened but rather ran homeward without once stopping.

Reaching home, he shut and locked all the doors, and then spread the handkerchief on the dirt floor as the holy man had instructed. Lo! a pile of gold coins appeared!

He repeated the process just to see if the handkerchief really was genuine, and again a pile of coins appeared. He called his wife and children. They were astonished at seeing the pile of gold coins. The poor man made the handkerchief perform and, of course, from that time on they did not doubt the poor man's word. Within a short time he bought a large estate and passed his days in uninterrupted happiness.

We could end our story here, but unfortunately, life is not like a folktale that ends happily.

The magic power of the handkerchief became known throughout the country. The king heard about the enormous wealth accumulated by the poor man simply by spreading a magic handkerchief on the ground, and he feared that the poor man would soon have more money than he. So the jealous king conceived a plan whereby he could gain possession of the handkerchief.

He sent a chamberlain to the wealthy landlord's estate. We can no longer call the poor man poor, so we shall call him wealthy landlord instead. The chamberlain praised the wealth and piety of the landlord. He also suggested that if the landlord so desired, his eldest son could become the husband of the king's daughter.

Now, to be the father-in-law of a princess was indeed a great honor. The landlord immediately sent a proposal of marriage to the king.

Next day, the chamberlain returned to the landlord and said that the king was pleased with the proposal, but wished to hear it from the lips of the landlord himself. The chamberlain also requested that the magic handkerchief be brought along, because the princess was eager to see its wondrous powers.

The wealthy landlord was received warmly by the king and his court. The king talked politely for a while and then asked if he might take the handkerchief to his daughter. The landlord, without suspecting anything, gave the handkerchief to the king.

Hours passed but no one returned. Finally, the landlord sent a message to the king kindly asking him to return the handkerchief. The king denied that he had ever seen it, and the landlord was driven from the palace. Showing no sign of anger, the landlord quietly went home, got his magic stick and returned to the palace gates, where he uttered these words:

Stick, stick, holy man's stick,
Beat them, beat them hard and quick,
Teach these people that greed is wrong,
Show them right is always strong!

The stick began its work. The queen was driven from one corner of her room to the other. The king was forced to crawl under his bed, but, of course, the magic stick followed him and continued its pommeling. The whole court was beaten. Such a scene of disorder was created that words fail to describe it.

Finally, the king, in anguish and pain, fell at the feet of the landlord and begged for mercy.

The landlord retrieved his magic handkerchief
and went home.

Day by day the landlord's wealth increased. He
lived happily to a ripe old age, and one day his
eldest son became king of the country.

The poor weaver and the princess

There was once a miserable weaver who could not make a decent living because his fellow villagers were too poor to buy his cloth. A compassionate and clever jackal who lived near-by came to the weaver's hut one day and said, "My dear friend, what if you could marry the king's daughter?"

The weaver merely smiled at this ridiculous idea and continued his work.

"Aha! You don't believe me. Well, my friend, I will make the impossible happen. You are a good man and deserve a better life."

The next day the jackal trotted off on his impossible mission. As it happened, he passed through a grove of betel plants. The leaves of this plant are a rare delicacy. The jackal, whose

mind worked very quickly, picked a bushel of
leaves and continued on his way to the king's
palace.

He placed himself at the edge of an enormous
blue pool, where the princess came to bathe. In
the late afternoon she came there with her attendants. The jackal spread the leaves on the grass
and began to munch on them.

"How unusual for a mere jackal to be eating
betel leaves," the surprised princess exclaimed.
"Even the wealthy in our land cannot afford them.
Tell me, sir jackal, is your country a paradise?"

The jackal made a sweeping bow. "Your Highness, in my country all people and all animals eat
betel leaves whenever they wish. Truly, it is a
paradise. And all the other goods things of life
are equally abundant."

"Ah, and what pleasure it must be for a king
to rule over such a contented place," sighed the
princess.

"Yes, truly. My king has so much money that
he grows weary counting it. But, alas, his happiness is not complete, because he has not found
a wife suitable to him. Many lovely princesses

have come to him, hoping that he would choose them. None were successful."

This piece of information excited the princess greatly. "He is not married?" she asked.

The jackal shook his head and continued eating the betel leaves. The princess rushed off to tell her parents the news, and soon a servant came to the jackal and escorted him to the throne room.

"Gaze upon my daughter, kind jackal," said the queen. "Is she not beautiful?"

"Indeed, she is. Even my king would be impressed with her," replied the shrewd jackal.

"I should think so!" said the queen, quite offended. "A hundred fine princes have sought her hand. None of them, however, was worthy or rich enough. Your king, I think, would make a perfect son-in-law. He is wealthy and knows what he wants. Could you persuade him to marry our daughter?"

"Your Highness, I will try, but I promise nothing."

The jackal left the palace in high spirits, chuckling over his success. A few hours later he was in the weaver's hut.

"My friend, you are no longer a poor man; you

84

are about to marry a beautiful princess and spend the rest of your life in the midst of luxury. But you must do as I tell you, or our lives are worth nothing."

The weaver was too overcome to speak. He listened to every word the jackal said and nodded his head. When the jackal finished outlining his plot, he returned to the king's palace. The royal couple was eager to receive him.

"Oh, it was terribly hard to convince him," said the jackal, feigning great weariness. "But I drew such a lovely picture of the princess that he could not resist. It took many hours, but he finally agreed to the marriage."

The king and queen and princess heaved a sigh of relief.

"Now, there is just one problem," said the calculating jackal. "If my king came here with all his attendants and elephants and maidservants and horses, you would have to build a new city to house them all. It is better, therefore, that he come with just a few friends and servants."

The wedding date was set, and the jackal once more took his leave.

Now, the shrewd jackal realized that the weaver

would not make a striking impression on his future bride and her parents. He did not even have a decent suit. So the jackal devised a plan. He went to the king of the jackals and requested one thousand jackals to accompany him to a spot near the king's palace. Then he went to the king of the crows and asked for a thousand crows. Finally he made the same request of the king of the cranes.

Early in the morning on the day of the wedding, the weaver and the jackal started out, accompanied by one thousand jackals, one thousand crows, and one thousand cranes.

When this impressive procession came within

a few miles of the palace, the jackal ordered his
fellow jackals to laugh, the crows to screech, and
the cranes to scream. The racket, as well can be
imagined, was deafening. While all this noise was
filling the air, the jackal rushed to the king's
palace and announced with a grand flourish,
"Your Highness, my king and his small wedding
party are arriving at the south gates."

The king was horrified. "Good heavens! There
must be ten thousand persons in the party. We
have no room in our city. Please beg your master
to come alone. We will offer him every luxury."

The jackal, pleased that his plan had worked
so well, said, "My master is an understanding

man, and he will come alone as you wish." And off he went to rejoin the weaver.

The thousand crows and the thousand cranes flew homeward while the jackals trotted after them. The weaver and the jackal entered the palace gates, and the weaver had a difficult time not showing his astonishment. Never before had he seen so much wealth.

The royal assemblage was shocked at the weaver's poor appearance, but the jackal quickly assured them that his master was a humble man who did not want to flaunt his wealth. So the wedding ceremony proceeded in all its pomp and splendor. The weaver, following the jackal's instructions, said very little, for fear that his common speech would give him away.

That night, as the weaver lay dreaming, he spoke out in his sleep. "Tomorrow I must repair my loom and begin working."

The princess overheard this and was horrified. This king whom she had married was talking like a common weaver. The next morning she told her parents about this strange experience.

The jackal was summoned to give an explanation. "Ah, my dear friends," said the witty jackal, "the answer is a simple one. My master has given acres and acres of land to the six hundred best weavers in the world. And being very interested in their art, he has learned the trade for his own amusement."

This clever explanation satisfied the princess and her royal parents, but the jackal was worried lest the weaver betray himself again. He convinced the king and queen that his master must return home in order to tend to affairs of state. A few days later the weaver, his wife, and the jackal set out for home.

When they arrived at the weaver's humble hut the jackal said, "My lovely bride, here is your husband's palace."

The poor princess moaned and beat her head against the door. "Ah, death would have been better than this," she wailed.

But the young wife was a good wife and quickly overcame her grief. She remembered what an old nursemaid had told her long ago, the secret of becoming rich.

She told the jackal to bring her a quantity of

flour. She added water to the flour and smeared it all over her body. As the paste dried, it began to flake off and drop, and as it dropped, it turned into gold. This process was repeated for many weeks until a quantity of gold, such as the world had never seen, was acquired.

An army of builders was employed and soon where the weaver's humble hut had stood, arose a beautiful and spacious palace. Six hundred weavers were settled around the palace. When all this was accomplished, the princess invited her parents to visit her.

The poor people of the village were given fine clothes, flower petals were strewn over the streets, the sick were given care—all this in preparation for the visit of the king and queen. They were overwhelmed with the display of wealth. As they entered the palace gates, the clever jackal leaped from behind a betel plant, bowed low and said, "Did I not tell you so?"

The man who was only three inches tall

One day in a Pakistan village, the people left their work and gathered at the well. They were very excited because an amazing thing had happened that morning. The woodcutter's wife had given birth to a fully developed man. The man could speak his native tongue perfectly. He could walk and run and leap. A long strand of black hair flowed down his back and trailed two feet behind him. But this was not the strangest thing about him. The strangest thing was that the man was only three inches tall!

How did this terrible event come about? It seems that for many years the woodcutter's wife could have no children. She and her husband prayed long and often to the goddess who gives

91

children, and they offered many beautiful gifts to her. At last, the goddess appeared before the unhappy couple. She gave the wife a cucumber and said that in seven days the wife should eat the cucumber whole, and then she would be blessed with a child. But the woodcutter's wife was so excited that she ate the cucumber the next day. The magic spell was broken; and, instead of a lovely baby, the wife gave birth to this strange man three inches tall.

While the villagers were gathered at the well excitedly discussing this amazing event, the little man passed by. He was searching for his father, who had fled into the woods soon after the strange birth. The villagers got down on their hands and knees to catch a better glimpse of the odd little fellow. He paid no attention to them. A grasshopper blocked his path. He nimbly scrambled over its back and entered the forest.

Soon he found his father furiously sawing a thick tree. The woodcutter sat down when he saw his son and buried his head in his hands.

"Ah, see what trouble you have caused me, ugly one. When you came into the world, I was so

miserable that I sold myself to the king. And now
I am a slave and cannot go home to my wife."

The little man, whom we shall call Three Inch,
left his father and went to the king's palace. He
begged the king to free his father, but the king,
who could not stand ugliness, turned his back on
Three Inch and declared, "I will not free your
father unless you bring me ten thousand rupees."

Plucky Three Inch immediately set forth to
collect this enormous sum. He came to a wide
river and leaned against a root, trying to devise
some way to get across. He gazed upward and lo!

a black cloud appeared just over his head. Three Inch, thinking that a thunderstorm was coming, started to run for shelter when he felt a tug on his strand of hair. He whirled around and there before him stood a smiling frog. There was no black cloud in the sky. Three Inch had simply gazed into the frog's bulging stomach. The friendly frog laughed and said, "I have heard that you are a woodcutter's son. If this is so, you must carry an ax. Down the road lives a blacksmith who will sell you an ax for one rupee."

Of course, Three Inch did not have a rupee, but he was a plucky fellow and started off to find the blacksmith. What a surprise! When Three Inch entered the yard, he discovered that the blacksmith was tinier than himself and had a beard four feet long! The blacksmith did not see Three Inch enter, and the latter saw a chance for some fun.

He crept up behind the blacksmith and tied his beard around the trunk of a tree. The blacksmith, unaware of his predicament, started to walk away. He tripped over his beard, jerked it, and fell flat on his face. Three Inch rolled on the ground, laughing. Of course, the blacksmith flew into a rage.

"Now, don't be upset," said Three Inch. "I am just a young lad who enjoys a practical joke. I will make a bargain with you. If you let me borrow your ax for a few days, I will untie your beard."

The blacksmith, realizing that he was in no position to argue, agreed. Three Inch, with ax in hand, ran back to the friendly frog.

"Now, Three Inch, you are a proper woodcutter's son. Wouldn't you like to use your ax? My wife is locked up in this oak tree. If you chop it down, she will be freed."

Three Inch promptly began chopping down the tree, and sure enough, there sat the frog's wife. The frog was so happy to be reunited with his mate that he gave Three Inch a tiny flask of green liquid.

"Take this to the king. He has a beautiful daughter who is blind. This liquid will cure her."

Three Inch thanked the frog and ran to the palace without stopping once. He marched up to the king's throne and said, "Your Majesty, I hear that you have a very lovely daughter. I wish to marry her."

The king's mouth dropped open. He was too amazed to be angry at Three Inch's impertinence.

"I would like very much for my daughter to get married. But this cannot happen until the bodies of the eight notorious thieves who dwell beyond the twelve rivers are brought to me."

Three Inch was not to be defeated. That very night he started on the journey across the twelve rivers. At daybreak, he found the eight thieves sitting around a campfire, counting their stolen money.

Three Inch climbed upon an ant hill and addressed them, "Dear gentlemen, I have come from the king who lives across the twelve rivers. He is eager for his beautiful daughter to be married. Since you are all wealthy men, he desires that you come to the palace; and he will choose one of you to be the lucky bridegroom."

The unsuspecting thieves happily agreed and followed Three Inch to the king's palace. Once inside the royal gates, Three Inch said that the king would see the thieves one by one. He told them to pass under a low tree and enter the throne room on the other side. Then, excusing himself, Three Inch climbed the low tree, and as each thief walked under it, he chopped off his head.

When the king saw the bodies of the eight thieves, he realized what a clever and brave fellow Three Inch was, in spite of his ugliness. The king could hold out no longer and agreed to the marriage.

And on the wedding day a wondrous thing happened. Three Inch produced the flask of green liquid and rubbed some on the daughter's eyes. In a flash her sight was restored. The whole kingdom rejoiced, and the king knew for sure that nowhere in the world could he find a more worthy son-in-law.

The king freed Three Inch's father and invited him and his wife to live in the palace. Soon Three Inch's parents learned to love him and were proud to claim him as their son.

Toontoony and the barber

Once upon a time, there was a warbling toontoony bird who lived in a tree in the garden of a king. It happened that one day while eating plums, a small plum-tree thorn caught in Toontoony's throat.

Unable to bear the pain, Toontoony flew to the village barber and said:

> O barber, Mr. Barber, see!
> Toontoony is in danger great!
> With pincers, pliers ready be
> To take the thorn out quick and straight!

98

Now the barber had been chosen to shave the king. Naturally, he was proud of his position. He sneered at Toontoony and said, "Who do you think you are? I am Mr. Barber of the royal family. I shave the king and cut his hair. You are a mere bird. *I* take out your thorn? Go elsewhere, silly bird."

Toontoony was fuming. I'll teach you a lesson, Mr. Barber, he thought to himself. So he flew to the king and pleaded:

> O King, O honored ruler, see!
> Toontoony is in danger great!
> The barber will not help poor me,
> Please punish him quick and straight!

The king did not even see Toontoony at first; and when he heard a little voice addressing him and finally saw the tiny bird, he burst into laughter. And he would not stop laughing. So Toontoony, in disgust, flew away to the home of a mouse.

> O mouse, Mr. Mouse, just see!
> Toontoony is in danger great!
> The barber will not help poor me,
> The king won't punish quick and straight.
> Tonight when the king is fast asleep,

99

Into his royal chambers creep,
And claw his stomach hard and deep!

The mouse bit his tongue to show that he was sorry for Toontoony, but said that it was impossible for him to scratch the king's belly.

Toontoony flew angrily away to the house of a cat.

Dear Auntie Cat, just look and see!
Toontoony is in danger great!
The barber will not help poor me,
The king won't punish quick and straight.
The mouse won't scratch the king's belly,
So eat the mouse, I say to thee!

The cat felt drowsy and flatly refused to catch the mouse.

What a predicament!

Toontoony flew to a stick and said:

Good stick, good stick, just look and see!
Toontoony is in danger great!
The barber will not help poor me,
The king won't punish quick and straight,
The mouse won't scratch upon my plea,
The cat won't eat him. What a state!
So please get up and start to beat
The drowsy cat and change my fate!

The stick replied, "Why should I beat the cat? She has done me no harm."

Poor Toontoony. He flew to the fire and cried:

> O roaring fire, just look and see!
> Toontoony is in danger great!
> The barber will not help poor me,
> The king won't punish quick and straight,
> The mouse won't scratch upon my plea,
> The cat won't eat him. What a state!
> The stick won't touch the cat, not he,
> So burn the stick in the fiery grate!

The fire replied, "Ah, me, I have burnt many things today, and I am tired. Please excuse me."

Rebuked again, Toontoony flew to the river.

> O powerful river, look and see!
> Toontoony is in danger great!
> The barber will not help poor me,
> The king won't punish quick and straight,
> The mouse won't scratch upon my plea,
> The cat won't eat him. What a state!
> The stick won't touch the cat, not he,
> Fire won't burn stick in the grate,
> So douse the fire for eternity!

But the river flowed by without even answering

poor Toontoony. So he flew to an elephant and said:

> O mighty elephant, look and see!
> Toontoony is in danger great!
> The barber will not help poor me,
> The king won't punish quick and straight,
> The mouse won't scratch upon my plea,
> The cat won't eat him. What a state!
> The stick won't touch the cat, not he,
> Fire won't burn stick in the grate,
> River won't douse fire for eternity,
> So drink the river that I hate!

The elephant replied that if he drank all the water in the river, his stomach would burst.

In desperation, Toontoony flew to a swarm of mosquitoes and cried out:

> Mosquitoes, mosquitoes, look and see!
> Toontoony is in danger great!
> The barber will not help poor me,
> The king won't punish quick and straight,
> The mouse won't scratch upon my plea,
> The cat won't eat him. What a state!
> The stick won't touch the cat, not he,
> Fire won't burn stick in the grate,
> River won't douse fire for eternity,
> Elephant won't drink river that I hate,

The plum thorn pains me more and more,
Go bite the elephant until he's sore!

The swarm of mosquitoes readily agreed to attack the elephant. They gathered together all the mosquitoes in the country. There were so many of them that they completely covered the elephant's hide. The elephant was so frightened that he promised Toontoony to drink up the river. And

The river promised to put out the fire,
The fire promised to burn the stick,
The stick promised to beat the cat,
The cat promised to eat the mouse,
The mouse promised to scratch the king,
The king promised to punish the barber,
The barber removed the thorn

And finally Toontoony was relieved of his pain.

The clever jackal and how he outwitted the tiger

Once upon a time a ferocious tiger, charging through the forest, was caught in a trap. He twisted and turned and strained, but he could not free himself. Along came a poor Brahmin.

The tiger cried out, "Oh, Brahmin, holy one, please get me out of this trap."

"I know you, man-eating tiger. If I set you free, you will devour me," said the Brahmin.

The tiger swore that he would not harm the pious Brahmin. The heart of the Brahmin softened, and he freed the tiger.

Immediately the ungrateful tiger pounced on him. "I have been hungry for many hours. I think that you will make a tasty dish."

The Brahmin begged for his life but to no avail.

104

Finally he said, "Tiger, let us make a bargain. I will ask three things whether or not they think that your actions are just. If they say yes, then you may eat me; if they say no, then you must spare my life."

The tiger, who enjoyed playing games, agreed.

The Brahmin first questioned an oak tree. Here is what the tree answered: "What is justice, Brahmin: All day long I offer shade to passing strangers, and how do they return my kindness? Why, by cutting off my branches and using them for kindling. It does me no good to complain, so why should you?"

The poor Brahmin was terribly upset by this answer. He wandered on and found a buffalo plodding in circles, turning a wheel that drew water from a well. But the Brahmin found no sympathy here either.

The buffalo said, "What is gratitude? When I give good milk, my master feeds me the finest food; but when I go dry, he chains me to this wheel, and all day long I must walk in circles and eat rubbish."

The Brahmin felt alone in the world. Soon the

tiger would eat him alive. There was no hope. Dejectedly, he asked the road to give its opinion. The road snarled and replied, "There is no justice or gratitude in this life. Every day I serve people. I make their way easier. And am I rewarded? No! Never! Don't complain. This is life."

On his way back to the tiger, the frightened Brahmin met a jackal. The jackal observed the great sadness in the holy man's eyes and asked, "Brahmin, what is the matter? You look as if the world were about to end."

"For me it is," replied the Brahmin, and then he told the jackal what had happened. The jackal shook his head. "I am very sorry, but I do not understand at all. Take me to the tiger and explain the whole thing over again."

When they found the tiger, he was sharpening his claws and licking his lips. "Well, Brahmin," said the tiger cruelly, "are you ready for dinner?"

"First grant me five minutes," said the Brahmin, trembling, "while I explain to the jackal what has happened."

The tiger growled his agreement. So the Brahmin related the story once more. The jackal scratched his head. "I just can't seem to remember anything today. Now, did you say that the tiger came along and found you in this trap and . . ."

"O you stupid jackal," howled the tiger. "*I* was in the trap."

"Now, let me see," said the jackal, scratching his head, "the trap was in the tiger and the Brahmin came walking by and . . ."

"No, no, no," cried the infuriated tiger. "*I* was in the trap. Look, I'm the tiger, right?"

"Right," replied the jackal.

"And this is the Brahmin."

"Right."

"And this is the trap, right?"

"Right."

"And my hind foot was caught in the trap, right?"

The jackal threw himself on the ground and pounded his head against a root. "My poor brain. It cannot understand. How were you in the trap?"

"Like this, you fool." And the tiger jumped into the trap and locked it.

"Ah," said the jackal gleefully, "I see. And since you seem to like it there so well, we'll just leave you in it."

And with that the Brahmin and the clever jackal bounded into the forest, laughing while the tiger twisted and turned and strained. Thereafter, the Brahmin did not doubt that there was justice and gratitude in this world.

The monkey, the tiger, and the jackal family

Once upon a time a jackal's wife gave birth to four cubs. The family had no shelter and so Mr. Jackal immediately set out to find a warm home. Fortunately, he soon found a wide, deep cave in the forest and took his family there. When they were all settled, Mr. Jackal went out in search of food.

Soon after her husband left, Mother Jackal saw a tiger approaching. Angrily the tiger demanded, "Who is that in my cave? Give me a quick answer."

Mother Jackal knew that she and her newborn cubs were in great danger. But what to do? She thought for a moment and came up with a clever plan.

The cubs were hungry and had been crying all day. Now Mother Jackal scolded them in a harsh voice. "Listen, you impatient children, didn't I say that your father is bringing home the head of a tiger for supper? Hush, soon we will have a great tiger feast."

When the tiger heard this, his heart began to thump loudly. He thought that some tiger-eating giants had taken shelter in his cave. Without thinking twice, he turned and dashed into the forest.

He met a monkey on the forest path who said, "Hello, Uncle, why are you running so fast? Who is chasing you?"

Without stopping, the tiger cried, "Nephew, some giants have taken shelter in my cave. They eat the heads of tigers for supper."

The monkey ran after him and told him to rest for a while. "I think that you have made a mistake," said the monkey. "Don't you know that you are the most powerful animal in the forest?"

But the tiger could not be comforted. The monkey suggested that the tiger go back to his cave and find out who was really there. But the tiger

said, "I'll be the last animal to go back, for there are tiger-eating giants in my cave."

Finally, after much persuasion, the tiger agreed to take a second look, but only if the monkey went with him. The monkey agreed and climbed onto the tiger's back. The tiger then asked his companion to tie their tails together so that the monkey could not run away if there was danger. The monkey tied their tails together, and then cautiously they made their way back to the cave.

In the meantime, Mr. Jackal had returned to the cave.

Mother Jackal peeked out of the cave and saw the tiger returning with the monkey on his back. She thought that death was surely near, and began thinking furiously of some trick that would stump the tiger. Suddenly she thought of one and whispered it to Mr. Jackal.

The tiger neared the cave with his heart thumping wildly. When he got within hearing distance, Mr. Jackal began pinching the four cubs; and they set up a terrific howl. Mother Jackal then shouted angrily, "I told you to bring home some tiger heads. Now see, our hungry cubs are crying. But wait! Look there! Isn't that a tiger coming? Take your gun and shoot him quickly."

Just at this moment, clever Mother Jackal set off some firecrackers which sounded exactly like gunshots.

This was too much for the tiger to stand. In terror he ran through the woods, smashing small trees and bushes and dragging the poor monkey behind him. When the tiger reached the other side of the forest, he found the monkey still tied to his tail, but, alas, he was dead.

The tiger untied the monkey, held him in his

paws, and spoke tenderly to him, "Didn't I tell you that there were tiger-eating giants in my cave? And now they have killed you!"

The tiger thanked God one hundred times for saving his life and then left to find another forest home.

The tale of a Pakistan parrot

The story goes that one morning a poor bird hunter was tramping through the woods when he came upon a beautiful parrot. He captured it easily and took it home. His wife made ready to prepare the bird for supper. Just as she was about to bring the knife down on its neck, lo and behold! the parrot began to speak.

"Friends, take me to the king and sell me."

The bird hunter and his wife were astonished, but their ears had not deceived them, for the bird spoke again. "Take me to the king, and I shall make you rich."

That very afternoon, the bird hunter and his wife took the marvelous parrot to the king and offered to sell it. Now the king enjoyed beautiful things, and the parrot caught his eye.

"What is your price, bird hunter?"

"I shall let the parrot speak for itself," replied the bird hunter.

"Eight thousand rupees, Your Majesty. That is a fair price, is it not?" said the parrot.

The king was so astonished to hear a bird speak, that he was struck dumb for several minutes. Finally he said, "If this is a trick, parrot, off goes your lovely head. If not, you will make a valuable companion for me."

The sum of eight thousand rupees was given to the fortunate bird hunter. He and his wife danced all the way home.

Now the king was so pleased to have a talking bird around the palace that he neglected everything else, including his six queens. The parrot spoke sensibly on all subjects and amazed the king by naming 330,000,000 gods of the Hindu religion. The parrot became the king's constant companion, and soon the six queens, their jealousy overflowing, plotted to kill the unique bird.

Their chance came when the king traveled to a neighboring kingdom on urgent business and left the parrot alone in his cage. The six queens had decided to ask the parrot which one of them was the ugliest, and when he named one of them, they were going to kill him because of his impertinence. But before they had a chance to ask, the

115

parrot began reciting the names of the 330,000,000 gods in the Hindu pantheon. The queens were so warmed by the parrot's piety that they left without accomplishing their evil plot.

Soon, however, their jealousy gave them fresh determination. They approached the parrot and asked, "Parrot, we know that you are an unusually intelligent bird. Could you tell us which one of us is the ugliest?"

Now the parrot knew that the intentions of the queens were not honorable, so he shrewdly answered, "Here I am locked up in this cage. I cannot answer your question fairly unless I examine each of you more closely."

The queens closed all the windows and doors. Then they freed the parrot. He walked slowly around each queen, pretending to examine her. Really he was looking for a way to escape. He caught sight of a crack in the wall and slowly moved toward it.

"My fair queens," he said, "there is a woman who lives beyond the four oceans and seven rivers. Not one of you can match her beauty."

Their vanity injured, the six queens rushed at

the defenseless parrot, but the clever bird evaded them and slipped through the crack in the wall.

When the king returned and found that his precious parrot was missing, he wept for days on end. A great reward was offered and, again, it was the lucky bird hunter who found the parrot and returned the bird to the palace.

When the parrot told the king about the six queens' evil plot, they were banished from the kingdom forever!

One day the king was sitting in his chambers with the parrot at his side. "Parrot, you told the evil queens about a woman whose beauty was unsurpassable. Was this true, and if so, can you take me to her?"

"The lady does exist, Your Majesty. And if you follow my instructions, she will be yours."

The parrot said that two things were necessary before they could begin the long trip. One was a winged horse, the other a quantity of silver buttons. In a short time all the arrangements were made. The king mounted his winged steed, with the parrot perched on his shoulder.

"One thing before we start," said the parrot.

"You must use your whip on the horse only once. If you strike him more than once, we will be stranded halfway between here and the beautiful lady. When we begin our homeward journey, again you must whip the horse only once."

The king nodded and touched the horse lightly with his whip. The steed sprang away from earth and soared high into the night sky. They sped across the four oceans and seven rivers, and twenty-four hours later they touched ground near the beautiful lady's palace.

According to the parrot's instructions, the king hid in a thicket. The parrot then took the silver buttons and dropping one every few feet, made a path to the palace gate.

Before long the lovely lady, dressed in a gown of rich crimson, strolled outside to catch a breath of cool night air. She discovered a silver button and saw another shining in the moonlight a few feet beyond. Her curiosity aroused, she followed the button path until she came to the thicket.

The king sprang from his hiding place and carried the lady off to where the parrot and the winged horse were waiting. With one touch from

the king's whip, the horse spread his wings and carried them into the black night. But the king was so eager to reach home with his exquisite prize that he whipped the horse a second time. Immediately the horse folded his wings and floated into a thick forest.

"Oh, my king," cried the parrot, "see what you have done! Why did you not heed my warning? It will take six months for the steed to regain his powers of flight, and that will happen only if he is fed the finest grains."

The stranded trio sat in the lonely forest, moaning over their misfortune, and finally fell into a deep slumber.

Now it happened that the prince of this country was hunting deer in the forest and came upon the sleeping strangers. He was captivated by the woman's beauty and ordered his servants to carry her off to his palace. But he seized the parrot's good master and put his eyes out!

Meanwhile, the helpless parrot hid high in the branches of a tree and waited for the hunting party to leave. His only thought was to stay by the king's side and make his lonely life in the forest as comfortable as possible.

The beautiful lady, snatched from her lover by the cruel prince, soon proved that she possessed more virtues than mere beauty. She begged the prince for one small favor—to keep the horse near her always. The prince saw no harm in this. A stable was built and the finest grains were put in the trough. Six months passed and the horse regained his strength.

The problem now was how to contact the parrot. The lovely lady could not leave the palace grounds, and there was no one around that she could trust. Suddenly an idea came to her. She pretended to have a deep love for birds, and each morning a large quantity of grain was spread on the flat roof of her house to attract them. Each day flocks and flocks of gorgeously plumed birds came to eat her dainties. She sat all day and watched them, hoping to find the parrot.

Meanwhile, the life of the king and his parrot had become dull and monotonous. All day they wandered through the forest. The faithful parrot gathered fruit for the king. At night they slept on soft pine needles. One day a flock of birds stopped to drink at a pool where the parrot was busy plucking plums for his master's dinner.

"Oh, parrot," sang the birds in unison, "leave your labor and spend the day with us. Every morning a kind lady sprinkles her roof top with the finest grains. Thousands of us go there. It is said that our beauty gives her great pleasure. Surely she would find you pleasing."

The parrot rejoiced at this news, because he shrewdly guessed who the kind lady was. Sure enough, when he reached the roof he found the lovely lady, and she immediately took him to her private chamber.

They talked for many hours and devised a plan of escape. "Now, my dear parrot, the most serious problem is not solved. The king is still blind. There is a tree near my garden gate beyond the four oceans and seven rivers. Go and gather the droppings of the green-and-purple birds that nest there."

The parrot flew away on his errand of mercy.

He returned a day later with the precious healing salve and applied it to his master's eyes.

Meanwhile, the lovely lady had escaped from the palace on the winged horse, and when the king opened his eyes the first thing he saw was his beautiful bride-to-be dressed in a white gown.

The happy trio mounted the winged horse and soon arrived at the king's palace. There was feasting and celebration for many days. The king and his lovely wife lived happily ever after, with the faithful parrot always at their side.

The crow and the grain of corn

Once upon a time a farmer's wife was sorting a basket of corn, looking for bad grains, when a crow swooped down, snatched one grain, and flew to a high branch in a tree near-by. The farmer's wife was enraged. She screamed so loudly at the crow that his beak dropped open and the grain of corn fell to the ground and rolled into a crack at the base of the tree.

"Find my grain of corn, Mr. Crow, or I'll chop off your head," cried the farmer's wife. The poor crow tried to reach the grain, but it had rolled too far into the tree trunk. He flew into the forest to find a woodcutter.

> Woodman! Woodman! Cut down the tree,
> I must get the grain of corn
> To save my life from the farmer's wife!

But the woodcutter refused to cut down the tree, so the frightened crow flew to the king's palace.

124

King! King! Kill the man
Who won't cut the tree
So that I can get the grain of corn
To save my life from the farmer's wife.

The king refused to kill the woodcutter, so the crow flew to the queen and pleaded:

Queen! Queen! Coax the king
To kill the man
Who won't cut the tree
So that I can get the grain of corn
To save my life from the farmer's wife.

But the queen would not coax the king, so the crow flew into the woods, where he met a snake.

Snake! Snake! Bite the queen
Who won't coax the king
To kill the man
Who won't cut the tree
So that I can get the grain of corn
And save my life from the farmer's wife.

But the snake refused to bite the queen, so the crow turned to a stick and said:

Stick! Stick! Beat the snake!
The snake won't bite the queen
The queen won't coax the king
To kill the man

Who won't cut the tree
So that I can get the grain of corn
And save my life from the farmer's wife.

But the stick refused to beat the snake. The crow flew on until he came to a roaring fire.

Fire! Fire! Burn the stick!
It won't beat the snake
The snake won't bite the queen
The queen won't coax the king
To kill the man
Who won't cut the tree
So that I can get the grain of corn
And save my life from the farmer's wife.

But the fire refused to burn the stick. The crow found a pool of water and begged:

Water! Water! Quench the fire
That won't burn the stick
That won't beat the snake
That won't bite the queen
Who won't coax the king
To kill the man
Who won't cut the tree
So that I can get the grain of corn
And save my life from the farmer's wife.

The water refused to quench the fire, so the crow flew on until he met an ox.

Ox! Ox! Drink the water!
The water won't quench the fire
The fire won't burn the stick
The stick won't beat the snake
The snake won't bite the queen
The queen won't coax the king
To kill the man
Who won't cut the tree
So that I can get the grain of corn
And save my life from the farmer's wife.

But the ox refused to drink the water. The poor crow continued until he met a rope.

Rope! Rope! Tie the ox!
The ox won't drink the water
The water won't quench the fire
The fire won't burn the stick
The stick won't beat the snake
The snake won't bite the queen
The queen won't coax the king
To kill the man
Who won't cut the tree
So that I can get the grain of corn
And save my life from the farmer's wife.

The rope would not tie the ox, so the crow flew on until he met a mouse.

> Mouse! Mouse! Gnaw the rope!
> The rope won't tie the ox
> The ox won't drink the water
> The water won't quench the fire
> The fire won't burn the stick
> The stick won't beat the snake
> The snake won't bite the queen
> The queen won't coax the king
> To kill the man
> Who won't cut the tree
> So that I can get the grain of corn
> And save my life from the farmer's wife.

The mouse would not gnaw the rope, so the crow flew on until he found a cat.

> Cat! Cat! Eat the mouse!
> The mouse won't gnaw the rope
> The rope won't tie the ox
> The ox won't drink the water
> The water won't quench the fire
> The fire won't burn the stick
> The stick won't beat the snake
> The snake won't bite the queen
> The queen won't coax the king

To kill the man
Who won't cut the tree
So that I can get the grain of corn
And save my life from the farmer's wife.

Now, never in this world has a cat refused to
eat a mouse.

So the cat caught the mouse
The mouse gnawed the rope
The rope tied the ox
The ox began to drink the water
The water began to quench the fire
The fire began to burn the stick
The stick began to beat the snake
The snake bit the queen
The queen coaxed the king
To harm the woodsman.
So, the woodsman cut down the tree
And the crow found the grain of corn
That saved his life from the farmer's wife.

The jackal with the torn nose

Once upon a time in a country far away, there lived an extremely clever jackal. One day he became very hungry and found a plum tree laden with fruit. Unfortunately, while he was eating with great relish, a thorn pierced his nose.

The pain was so terrible that he hastened to the village barber, who was skilled in removing thorns. The barber was sitting in his chambers smoking a hookah when he heard the jackal's cry.

"Mr. Barber, are you there? If so, please come quickly; a patient is in danger."

Since the barber was serious about his profession, he rushed outside, carrying his bag of instruments. But while removing the thorn with the *narun,* a nail-cutter made of iron, the barber slipped and severely cut the jackal's nose. The jackal became so furious that he threatened to bite the barber. The poor barber apologized a
130

hundred times and finally gave the *narun* to the jackal in order to pacify his anger.

A torn nose can never be mended, and something is better than nothing; so the jackal, grumbling and muttering, accepted the gift and went on his way.

He had not walked far when he saw a potter digging in the earth with his bare hands. The potter needed clay to make earthenware pitchers and jugs and plates; but as there was no blacksmith near-by, he could not get a spade to make the digging easier. The potter asked the jackal to lend him the *narun* for a few minutes. The jackal gave it to the potter. It was a very delicate instrument and was broken right away.

The jackal began to boil with rage and was ready to bite the potter with his poisonous teeth. The potter made a thousand apologies and offered the jackal an earthen pitcher.

Something is better than nothing, thought the jackal. So he accepted it and went on his way.

Coming to a curve in the road, he saw a bridal procession approaching. There were musicians playing and drums beating and fireworks explod-

ing in red-and-blue flashes. One of the firecrackers accidentally fell into the jackal's pitcher, exploded, and shattered it into a thousand pieces.

The jackal was furious beyond words. He started toward the bridegroom and was going to bite and kill him instantly. At this, the bridal party became so upset that they offered to give the bride away in order to get rid of the angry jackal.

The bride was beautiful, and the jackal made up his mind to marry her. But to get married is not a trifling thing. One must have a band of musicians and a priest to say the incantation.

The jackal hastened to a musician's house and called to him, but unfortunately he was not there. So the jackal left his bride-to-be with the drummer's wife and hurried off to find a priest.

The bride felt drowsy and fell asleep near the open hearth where the drummer's wife was cooking rice. While nodding in slumber, the bride tumbled into the fire and was burned to death. The drummer's wife became terribly frightened. She moved the body to a secret place and then hid herself on the roof top because she was afraid of the jackal's wrath.

A short time later, the jackal returned with the priest. But where was the bride? She could not be found anywhere. The jackal raged and demanded to know where his bride-to-be was. Otherwise, he threatened to set the house on fire.

The poor drummer's wife began to shake like a reed. With clasped hands she narrated the whole

133

story from her hiding place, all the while pleading her innocence and begging the jackal's forgiveness.

The jackal still raged and stormed and would not listen to her appeal.

Finally he said that he would forgive her if she gave him one of her husband's finest drums. In order to spare her own life, the drummer's wife immediately handed the jackal a fine drum and he went on his way.

With the drum tied around his waist, the jackal climbed a palm tree which was in a lonely place. He began to beat the drum and to sing like this:

Tak dooma doom doom
Bravo!
Tak dooma doom doom.
My nose was cut by the barber
And I was given a *narun.*
Tak dooma doom doom.

The potter broke my *narun*
And gave me a pitcher instead.
Tak dooma doom doom
Bravo!
Tak dooma doom doom.

The pitcher was shattered
And I received a bride.
Tak dooma doom doom
Bravo!
Tak dooma doom doom.

I lost my bride.
And was handed this drum.
Tak dooma doom doom
Hurrah!
Tak dooma doom doom.

Joyously and with great zeal the jackal was beating the drum and singing at the top of his lungs when suddenly he lost his balance and fell from the high, high tree.

And thus Mr. Jackal, for all his cunning, met a tragic end.

Four friends

Long, long ago in a certain country there lived a washerman who owned an old donkey. When the donkey became so old that he could no longer work, the washerman drove him from the house.

With a heartful of sorrow, the donkey plodded down the road. Nearing the village, he met an old dog. The dog was sprawled in the dirt; there was a sad expression on his face. The donkey asked, "Brother Dog, why do you look so dejected?"

The dog replied, "Ah, what can I say? Because I have become old and feeble, my master has driven me from the house."

The donkey consoled him by saying, "Such is the world. We work hard for our masters, and when we no longer are useful, they send us from the house."

The donkey invited the dog to travel with him,

and the friendless dog readily accepted. They had not gone far, when they encountered a cat. She was mewing pitifully. "What is the matter, Sister Cat?" the donkey asked kindly.

The cat wiped her eyes and replied, "What can I say? I am very old and cannot catch mice any more. Last night my master thrashed me and drove me from the house."

The dog bent his head in sympathy and said, "The same thing has happened to us. Men are such ungrateful creatures. Come, travel with us. You need companions at a time like this."

So the unhappy trio set off down the road. Soon they found a hen weeping by the roadside. Her feet were tied with a strong rope. The cat said, "Sister Hen, tell us what is the trouble?"

In a choked voice, the hen answered, "What can I say? I laid thousands of eggs for my master and presented thousands of chicks to him. Now that I am old and infirm, my master has decided to eat me."

"That is a woeful story," said the cat. "We also have encountered unhappiness." And one by one the donkey, the dog, and the cat narrated their stories. Then the cat gently untied the rope from the hen's feet and invited her to join them.

The four friends walked until evening when they found themselves at the edge of a forest. The cat with her sharp eyes peered into the foliage and spied a lighted house. She offered to go and investigate.

The cat crept up to the front window and discovered a gang of robbers. Around them was piled a treasure in gold and gems and other precious things. They were eating platters full of delicious food.

The cat ran back to her friends and told them what she had seen. Immediately the dog offered a plan. "Let us go back to the house. I have thought of a plan that will frighten the robbers out of their skin. Let me stand on the donkey's back. The cat will stand on the dog's back, and the hen will perch on the cat's head. Then we shall bark and meow and bray and scream at the top of our lungs."

The other three agreed that this was a fine plan,

and soon the four friends were standing on each other's back in front of the window. Then a great tumult was raised in the forest such as never had been heard before. Braying, crowing, barking, meowing mixed together to make a frightening noise. The robbers, thinking that they had been discovered, scattered into the forest and were never seen again.

The four friends moved into the house and spent their old age in luxury and contentment.

The old woman and the thief

Long, long, long ago, there lived in Bengal a very, very old woman. Her hair was the purest white. Her back was hunched, and she walked with her wrinkled face bent toward the ground. The old woman had nobody in the world, neither son nor daughter. Her most valued possession was a bamboo stick. She went from this village to that village, from this house to that house, begging food.

Due to her extreme age, the old woman became partially blind. In the nighttime she could see nothing at all. Taking advantage of this, a thief began coming at night to the old woman's room and stealing all the food which she had gathered that day.

The poor old woman questioned all the neighbors, but no one had seen the mysterious thief.

One morning, after the thief had carried off all

her food once more, the sad old woman was walking along the road with an empty bag in her hand. As always she was going somewhere to beg for food.

Suddenly a coconut fell from the top of a slowly swaying tree. The fruit rolled to the feet of the old woman, and lo and behold! it began to talk in a human voice.

"Old woman! Old woman! Put me in your bag! Who knows, but I may be able to serve you."

The old woman was sceptical. "How can this little thing help me? But my luck has been so bad lately, perhaps I should take it with me." So reluctantly she dropped it into her bag and continued on her way.

A little further down the road, she came to a beehive. The bees swarmed around her and said, "Old woman! Old woman! Put us in your bag! We may be able to serve you."

The old woman thought that the bees might sting her if she didn't put them in the bag, so she opened it and the whole beehive buzzed inside.

Further on, the old woman spied a knife lying in the dust. The knife spoke to her.

"Old woman! Old woman! Take me with you! Possibly I can be of help to you."

Ah, what help can you be to me, little thing, thought the old woman to herself, but she put the knife in her bag anyway.

She had not walked far, when an old cat rubbed up against her legs and said in a human voice, "Old woman! Old woman! Take me with you! Sometime I may be able to help you."

Yes, little creature, thought the old woman, perhaps you can help. Things can't get worse. And she dropped the cat into her bag.

At nightfall the old woman returned home. Before going to bed, she placed the coconut on the warm hearth so that it would become soft enough to eat the next morning. She hung the beehive on a hook near the door. She threw the knife on the floor. The cat curled up near the fire.

In the dead of night, the greedy thief entered the old woman's home and moved silently toward the hearth where always before he had found food. Just as he reached down to feel for the food, the old cat attacked him ferociously with her sharp claws. The thief, in his haste to get away, tripped and fell on the knife. He cut himself badly. He leaped up, stepped on the coconut, and twisted his ankle.

By this time, the bees were angered by the commotion. As the thief dragged himself out the door the bees swarmed upon him. His screams awakened all the neighbors, who rushed to the old woman's door and caught the thief red-handed.

How surprised and perplexed the neighbors were to see the old woman kiss the knife and the coconut, and hug the cat and the beehive. And they never did find out how this feeble old woman caught the thief.

The ruby prince

It happened one day that while walking along a country road, a poor Brahmin came upon a beautiful red stone glowing in the dust. The Brahmin, liking the sparkle of the stone, dropped it into his pocket and continued on his way. He was very hungry, and finding a roadside inn, offered to exchange the stone for food.

The proprietor saw immediately that the stone was a ruby worth a great fortune. But he was an honest man and said: "If I were you, sir, I would take this stone to the king. Only a king could pay what it is worth."

The Brahmin thanked the proprietor for his honest advice and proceeded to gain an audience with the king. His majesty tapped his fingers on the arm of his throne to show that he was bored

144

by the Brahmin's visit, but when the red stone was handed to him, he quickly sat upright and his eyes widened.

"Brahmin, what is your price?"

The Brahmin replied, "Your Majesty, I am a simple man and my needs are few. A bushel of corn for the winter would make me very happy."

The king clapped his hands. "A bushel of corn you shall have, Brahmin, and much more besides. This red stone is the most beautiful of my possessions, and you will be rewarded for bringing it to me."

The royal chests were brought before the king. A generous sum of money was given to the humble and happy Brahmin.

The queen placed the ruby in a velvet trunk under lock and key. And there it lay for many years, untouched, until one day the king's fancy turned toward the stone and he ordered it brought before him.

The queen was there, and all the courtiers. There was music in the royal hall and a low hum of conversation filled the air, but when the velvet

trunk was opened, a hush suddenly fell upon the
crowd. For out of the trunk stepped a strong and
very handsome young man!

The amazed king demanded, "Who are you,
and what have you done with my beautiful stone?"

"I am the Ruby Prince."

146

"Well, and just who is the Ruby Prince?"

"*I* am the Ruby Prince."

The king became angry at this silly answer and drove the young man from the palace. At the palace gates, a kindhearted soldier gave the young man a horse and weapons.

Just outside the village, the Ruby Prince found an old woman kneading bread and crying. Taking compassion, he asked gently, "Old woman, what trouble causes these tears to come?"

"Oh, kind sir, just on the other side of the village dwells a monster who lives on human flesh. Each month one of our fine young men is offered to the monster to pacify him. This month my son was chosen, and tomorrow he must die."

"Ah," said the Ruby Prince, "but if someone should kill this monster . . ."

"Then, kind sir, we would be free. But, alas, there is no one strong enough or daring enough."

"Have faith," replied the Ruby Prince. "Perhaps the strong, daring man has arrived."

All night the Ruby Prince waited for the monster, but the awesome creature did not show itself. At daybreak the monster emerged from his den, expecting to find a human feast. Seeing that the offering had not been delivered, the monster stomped and raged and prepared to revenge himself upon the village. Just then the Ruby Prince leaped out from behind a bush, and with his sharp sword cut off the monster's head and claws. He then hung them on the village gates to show the people that they no longer need fear the monster.

But when the village folk saw the sight, they were horrified. They thought that some trickster had hung a false head and false claws on the gate to enrage the dreaded monster. They ran straight to the king and told him what had happened.

The king went to the old woman's hut. She was sitting outside, rocking back and forth in glee.

"Old woman," said the king impatiently, "have you seen what hangs on our village gate? Is this a trick of yours to save your son? If so, the monster, in rage, will kill us all."

"No, my king, the monster really *is* dead, and inside, sleeping, lies the brave man who killed it."

The king's curiosity got the better of him. He entered the hut, and lo and behold! there lay the young man whom he had recently banished from the palace.

"Ruby Prince, awake and accept my apologies and our deepest gratitude. You deserve a reward equal to the greatness of your deed."

The king conferred briefly with his ministers and then announced, "I decree that the Ruby Prince shall have my daughter in marriage and shall rule half my kingdom."

The Ruby Prince and his princess were married in great pomp and luxury. For a while the young princess was extremely happy because everyone remembered her husband's heroism and accorded him great respect. But in the course of everyday life, valiant deeds are often forgotten. Soon the ladies-in-waiting began to gossip about the Ruby Prince's unknown origin. Who was he? Where did he come from?

The princess overheard the gossip and was consumed with a desire to have these questions answered. Every day she gently asked the Ruby Prince about his childhood, his home, and his father. And every day he gently answered, "Dear wife, do not ask me these questions. I cannot tell you."

The princess was a persistent soul. One day they were standing by the river that runs past the village. She took the Ruby Prince's arm tenderly in her hands and said, "Show your love for me, my husband. Tell me who you are."

The poor prince shook his head sorrowfully. "I cannot tell you," he said. And he stepped into the stream.

Still the willful young woman would not cease her questioning.

"Tell me where you came from, my husband."

The water rippled around the prince's shoulders. "That I cannot tell you," he said.

In frustration, the princess stamped her foot and screamed, "I want to know. Tell me! Tell me!"

And suddenly the Ruby Prince disappeared into the water, and from that spot emerged a bright green serpent whose scales were covered with jewels. It wore a golden crown, and there was a ruby stone in its forehead. For a few minutes, it looked with sad eyes upon the princess and then disappeared beneath the surface.

The distraught princess returned to the palace and wept all day for her lost prince and despised her willfulness. A large bag of gold was offered to anyone who saw the Ruby Prince or heard anything about him. Many days passed and there was no word. The princess languished in her tears.

Finally a servant woman came to the palace and related a strange tale. "I was gathering wood in the forest last evening. Growing drowsy, I lay down under a tree to rest. When I awoke, the forest was flooded in a strange light. It was neither moonlight nor sunlight, just a pale silver glow. As I rubbed my eyes in wonderment, a little man emerged from a snake's hole at my feet and spread a beautiful blue carpet on the ground. Then I heard music that seemed to come from deep in the earth, and soon a band of handsome, jeweled young men came out of the hole. They were only two inches tall. One man seemed to be their king. The others played and danced for him. All, that is, except one, who had a ruby stone in his forehead. He did not dance or sing, but sat and stared into the darkness."

The princess did not doubt that the moody young man was her beloved Ruby Prince. That night the servant woman led the princess to the snake's hole. They hid behind a bush and waited. First, the eerie light flooded the forest, then the blue carpet was spread by a tiny man, and finally the band of young men danced and sang their way out of the hole. All, that is, except one. And the heart of the princess leaped at seeing this one, for she recognized him as her lost husband.

Every night the princess slipped into the forest with the servant woman and watched the strange gathering. But her aching heart was not soothed, because she could not talk to her husband. The servant woman, seeing how unhappy the lovely princess was, suggested a plan.

"Notice, dear Princess, how much the young king enjoys the dancing. But is it not true that he has seen only men perform? Perhaps if a lovely young woman danced for him, he would be so overjoyed that he would grant her fondest wish."

And so it came about that the princess, after

practicing many days, became the most graceful
dancer in the kingdom.

The night came when she would dance before
the tiny king. She chose her finest veil and mus-
lins. Jewels sparkled in her hair. At midnight she
and the servant woman went into the woods.
Once again the strange light flooded the forest
and the blue carpet rolled away from the snake's
hole. The princess, in hiding, trembled with fear.
At last the young men emerged; the dancing and
music began. When all except the unhappy Ruby

Prince had cavorted before the king, the lovely princess leaped from her hiding place and began to dance.

The tiny king watched, spellbound. Never had he seen such dancing! As soon as the princess finished, the king sprang up and cried, "My lovely, unknown dancer who has thrilled my heart more than anyone before, name your wish. It will be yours."

"Your Majesty," replied the princess, "my dance was for the Ruby Prince. I wish to take him home with me."

The tiny king was not happy with this request. "I never allow my men to leave me, but I have promised. Take him and leave this place, never to return."

The Ruby Prince suddenly grew into his full stature. He and his beloved wife melted into the shadows. They lived happily together, and never again did the princess ask, "Who are you, my husband, and where did you come from?"

The storyteller

One day an elderly storyteller was sitting by the village well. Around him were gathered a group of young children listening intently to his every word. The story went like this:

"Once upon a time there lived a fowler. One day he went into the forest with his huge net and soon caught one hundred birds!"

The storyteller stopped and stared off into the distance. The children grew impatient and cried out, "Well, one hundred birds were caught in the fowler's net . . . that's very fortunate. But what happened then?"

The storyteller replied somewhat vaguely, "Yes, yes, I was just coming to that point. There were many kinds of birds in the net—such as the dove, nightingale, pigeon, parrot, crane, sparrow, warbler, and many others."

155

"Now," continued the storyteller, "do you know what happened next? A clever parrot cut a hole in the net with his beak and flew out. Then the dove, nightingale, pigeon, crane, sparrow, warbler, and all the other birds began to escape through the hole."

Again the storyteller paused as if he were waiting for something to happen.

The excited children could not wait any longer and exclaimed, "Yes, yes, the one hundred birds began to escape, and then what happened?"

The old storyteller seemed a trifle irritated, but he continued, "Yes, one parrot flew out of the hole and fluttered his wings which made a sound like this: *flippity-flip-flap-flip.* And the fowler ran after the bird. In the meantime, another bird came through the hole and fluttered his wings, *flippity-flip-flap-flip,* and the poor fowler began chasing that one. Then, *flippity-flip-flap-flip:*

> Flippity to the left,
> Flippity to the right,
> Flippity behind,
> And everywhere flippity!

For the third time, the storyteller stopped his tale.

The excited children clapped their hands and cried out, "Yes, yes, that's very interesting, but what happened then?"

"What happened then?" inquired the storyteller. "Why I shall come to that soon, but first we must let all the birds fly away."

"But they have flown away," cried out the children. "What happened next?" they cried in exasperation.

"No, children, wait, wait! You see there are still plenty of birds left that must fly through the hole. It will take some time."

Then the storyteller leaned back against the well and waited while the one hundred birds flew away.

Here my story ends:

The *notē* plant sways and bends,
"O *notē* plant, why do you sway?"
"Why does the cow eat at me, say?"
"O cow, why do you eat the *notē's* leaves?"
"Because the cowherd never sees "
"O cowherd, why don't you watch your herd?"
"Why doesn't the housewife give me
    food and curd?"
"O housewife, why don't you feed the lad?"
"Because the children cry and act so bad."
"O children, why do you weep and wail?"
"Why doesn't Grandma tell a tale?"
A tale, a tale, a tale . . .

Fairy Gold: A Book of Classic English Fairy Tales

Chosen by Ernest Rhys

Illustrated by Herbert Cole

"The Fairyland which you enter, through the golden door of this book, is pictured in tales and rhymes that have been told at one time or another to English children," begins this charming volume of favorite English fairy tales. Forty-nine imaginative black and white illustrations accompany thirty classic tales, including such beloved stories as "Jack and the Bean Stalk," "The Three Bears," and "Chicken Licken" (Chicken Little to American audiences). *Ages 9-12*

236 pages • 5 1/2 x 8 1/4 • 49 b/w illustrations • 0-7818-0700-X • W • $14.95hc • (790)

Folk Tales from Chile

Brenda Hughes

This selection of 15 tales gives a taste of the variety of Chile's rich folklore. There is a story of the spirit who lived in a volcano and kept his daughter imprisoned in the mountain, guarded by a devoted dwarf; there are domestic tales with luck favoring the poor and simple, and tales which tell how poppies first appeared in the cornfields and how the Big Stone in Lake Llanquihue came to be there. Fifteen charming illustrations accompany the text. *Ages 7-10*

121 pages • 5 1/2 x 8 1/4 • 15 illustrations • 0-7818-0712-3 • W • $12.50hc • (785)

Folk Tales from Russia

by Donald A. Mackenzie

From Hippocrene's classic folklore series comes this collection of short stories of myth, fable, and adventure—all infused with the rich and varied cultural identity of Russia. With nearly 200 pages and 8 full-page black-and-white illustrations, the reader will be charmed by these legendary folk tales that symbolically weave magical fantasy with the historic events of Russia's past. *Ages 9-12*

192 pages • 8 b/w illustrations • 5 1/2 x 8 1/4 • 0-7818-0696-8 • W• $12.50hc • (788)

Folk Tales from Simla

Alice Elizabeth Dracott

From Simla, once the summer capital of India under British rule, comes a charming collection of Himalayan folk lore, known for its beauty, wit, and mysticism. These 56 stories, fire-side tales of the hill-folk of Northern India, will surely delight readers of all ages. Eight illustrations by the author complete this delightful volume. *Ages 12 and up*

225 pages • 5 1/2 x 8 1/4 • 8 illustrations • 0-7818-0704-2 • W • $14.95hc • (794)

Folk Tales from Turkey

Collected by Dr. Ignacz Kunos, translated by R. Nisbet, illustrated by Celia Levetus

These 17 classic Turkish folk tales whisk the reader into a realm of romance, iniquity, suspense, and adventure. "The Piece of Liver," "The Rose-Beauty," and "The Ghost of the Spring and the Shrew," are just a few examples of the folk tales presented in this collection—each story uniquely weaving the important threads of Turkish customs, culture, and values with magic and fantasy, deeply rooted in Turkish tradition. Seven beautiful black-and-white line drawings bring these stories to life. *Ages 12 and up*

205 pages • 7 b/w line drawings • 5 1/2 x 8 1/4 • 0-7818-0697-6 • W• $14.95hc • (795)

All prices subject to change. **To purchase Hippocrene Books** contact your local bookstore, call (718) 454-2366, or write to: HIPPOCRENE BOOKS, 171 Madison Avenue, New York, NY 10016. Please enclose check or money order, adding $5.00 shipping (UPS) for the first book and $.50 for each additional book.